THE
GRAHAM
CRACKER
PLOT

THE GRAHAM CRACKER PLOT

SHELLEY TOUGAS

SQUARE
FISH

Roaring Brook Press
New York

SQUARE
FISH

An Imprint of Macmillan
175 Fifth Avenue
New York, NY 10010
mackids.com

Square Fish and the Square Fish logo are trademarks of Macmillan and
are used by Roaring Brook Press under license from Macmillan.

Square Fish books may be purchased for business or promotional use.
For information on bulk purchases, please contact the Macmillan Corporate
and Premium Sales Department at (800) 221-7945 x5442 or
by e-mail at specialmarkets@macmillan.com.

Library of Congress Cataloging-in-Publication Data

Tougas, Shelley.
    The graham cracker plot / Shelley Tougas.
        pages cm
    Summary: Calamity ensues when almost twelve-year-old Daisy and her
sometimes best friend Graham try to break Daisy's father out of prison.
    ISBN 978-1-250-06810-1 (paperback) — ISBN 978-1-59643-989-4
(ebook) [1. Friendship—Fiction. 2. Prisoners—Fiction. 3. Escapes—
Fiction. 4. Letters—Fiction.] I. Title.
    PZ7.T647155Gr 2014
    [Fic]—dc23

                                                    2014003236

"We did not dare to breathe a prayer," from The Ballad of Reading Gaol by
Oscar Wilde.

Originally published in the United States by Roaring Brook Press
First Square Fish Edition: 2015
Book designed by Andrew Arnold
Square Fish logo designed by Filomena Tuosto

10 9 8 7 6 5 4 3 2 1

AR: 3.8 / LEXILE: 550L

For Samantha, my little daisy

THE FIRST PART

DEAR JUDGE HENRY,

I will tell you three things right now.

Number one: I'm almost twelve years old. I do not want to go to prison, even if it's a prison for kids.

Number two: Nobody calls me Aurora Dawn Bauer, not even my grandma, and she's the most legal person I know. Everyone calls me Daisy.

Number three: Your face looks like squirrels flopped their tails where your eyebrows should be. I can't tell if your eyes ever laugh, but you were all business when you told me to write this, and—

UGH. Mom just peeked over my shoulder and said, "Erase that stuff about his weird eyebrows or we'll have more trouble. I mean it!" I went to my room and slammed the door. She's a snoop.

You told me to write everything I think and feel. *Everything*. And I will.

Mom's afraid. If I screw this up, she says, the County will never get off her back.

I won't screw it up. I'm going to do what you said and use the brain God gave me to explain myself instead of causing more trouble.

Mom thinks I could finish this paper in a couple of nights if I work hard. She has no idea how much I have to say. Sometimes you hold stuff tight inside until a judge makes you let it out, and the stuff starts a spark and the spark starts a fire and the fire burns big and terrible. The Chemist says you can't stop a big and terrible fire with a regular garden hose.

So who caused this mess? Not the Chemist. I swear on everything I'll ever have—every single Christmas present and birthday present from every single Christmas and birthday. The Chemist didn't know we were going to break him out of prison. It's not his fault.

You should blame my mom and her boyfriend, Alex, for running off to Mexico. Or Kari, the worst babysitter in the world. Or Grandma's crying. Or Ashley and that dog whose name may or may not be Fred. And most of all, you should blame my never-friend Graham Hassler, aka Graham Cracker, and his stupid Idea Coin. If you broke up this story into one million pieces of blame, only two of the pieces would be mine and 999,998 would belong to Graham.

Why do you think we called it the Graham Cracker Plot?

DEAR JUDGE HENRY,

The Chemist is my dad, but he's not the kind of dad who lives in your house. He doesn't drive me to school or fold socks or put away dishes. My parents were never married, so he didn't learn that stuff.

The Chemist's the kind of dad who buys presents and lets you watch zombie movies and gives you ice cream even though you already had cookies. Mom was like that, too, back when she'd put booze in a travel mug and pretend it was coffee. But now, she's all, "Eat your peas and do your homework and that's enough TV for one day."

So my dad and I were eating mozzarella sticks at the Rattlesnake Bar and Grill when we gave each other new names.

"Guess what I did at school today?" I said.

"Played with Graham?"

Nobody seemed to get the Graham thing. I said, "He's an after-school friend."

"What's that? A part-time friend? Like a part-time job?"

"We don't hang out at school." Something about Dad's face said, "Buckle up for a guilt trip. Poor Graham doesn't have a dad and goes to special reading classes and probably won't ever get braces for his crooked teeth." I wanted that look wiped off his face quick. I said, "Graham pulls my ponytail and makes fart noises with his armpit."

"Oh, come on. Armpit farts are hilarious." He laughed and laughed. Then he wiped his eyes on his napkin and said, "The ponytail thing means he likes you."

"Hello! I said I have a story to tell! Guess what I did at school today?"

"You took over the cafeteria from the crabby old ladies? And you threw away the veggies and made marshmallow sandwiches!"

"That'd be awesome. But, no. We were in the media center and we looked up our names to learn their meaning and where they came from. What were you thinking when you named me Aurora Dawn?"

He asked the waitress for two more beers—a real one for him and a root one for me. "Your mom picked Aurora, and her favorite aunt was named Dawn. It's a great name. It's unusual. Now my name? It sucks. Do you know how many Jacobs are in this world? Probably millions."

"Guess what? Aurora *means* the dawn! My name is Dawn Dawn! Do you know how dumb that sounds?"

He thought about it. "Really? Are you sure?"

"Yes! I found it on the Internet. I couldn't write that on my paper. *Dawn* Dawn. Dawn *Dawn*!"

"So what'd you say?"

"I wrote that it means Daisy."

"I gotta tell you sweetie, Daisy Dawn Bauer sounds pretty silly, too."

I shrugged. "Time was up, and I was thinking about the wallpaper in Grandma's bathroom with the little daisies. It's better than Dawn Dawn."

"Better than Jacob, too," he said. We tended to agree on most everything.

He pulled the last mozzarella stick in two pieces and gave me the bigger half. That's when I got the idea. "How about I go by Daisy, and you go by something that's like you. How about Video Game Man?"

"I do like video games. But it doesn't exactly roll off the tongue, does it, Daisy?"

"Carpet Cleaning Man!"

"I quit that job."

"Mom said the job quit you."

"She gets things mixed up, doesn't she?" He took a gulp of beer and said, "Well, I was good at chemistry in school. I took two chemistry classes before I left college, and I'm kinda into that."

"Chemistry Man?"

"The Chemist." He smiled. "Yeah. The Chemist."

* * *

A few months later, the Chemist went to prison. You weren't the judge who did that to us. I already asked Grandma, and she'd know because she paid the lawyer bills. If you were *that* judge, who punished my daddy for an accident, I'd use all the bad words I promised the Chemist I wouldn't say until high school.

DEAR JUDGE HENRY,

It was Graham's idea to run away. But it was Grandma's idea to break the Chemist out of Club Fed. That's what Grandma and the Chemist call the prison, and it's a joke, because it's not a club.

Judge Henry, you probably know that Club Fed doesn't look like a movie prison. No bars, no handcuffs. But did you know Club Fed used to be a small college, and when the college closed, the Club Fed people made it a low-security prison? I guess judges don't go to prisons on account of prisoners not liking judges. But you should go anyway, with your little desk hammer and black robe, to make sure bad prisoners don't beat up nice prisoners.

The first time I went to Club Fed with Grandma, I could hardly believe it. The prison looks like a college—just a bunch of brick buildings and a big lawn. Except it's surrounded by a fence.

Grandma is how I get to see the Chemist. Mom told Grandma it would scar me to see the Chemist in prison. Grandma said I'd be scarred if I didn't see him. Nobody asked what I thought, Judge Henry, but since you wagged your finger at me and said to tell you everything, I will! I thought, *Mom and Grandma should stop giving each other scars. Why'd it matter anymore whether Mom broke the Chemist's heart or whether the Chemist broke hers?*

Seems to me they both got broken. And that's what would happen to me if I couldn't see the Chemist. I'd be broken.

So Grandma got a lawyer and a legal paper that says I have to spend the third weekend of every month with her. We drive thirty miles to the prison in Waseca and see the Chemist.

Every time we go, Grandma reminds me killers don't go to Club Fed. No shooters, stabbers, or stranglers. The men at Club Fed didn't pay tax money and hacked into computers and accidentally blew up a house while mixing a chemistry experiment, like the Chemist.

Every time we go, Grandma laughs the whole time we're in the visiting center. Her eyes shine bright, and she tells funny stories about being a stylist.

And every time we leave, when it's just us in the car, she cries about how unfair it is. I ask why a judge would punish someone for an accident, and she just blows her nose and fixes her makeup. Then she puts on a happy face and says, "McDonald's time."

But our visit in March changed everything. It was so bad, so scary, that Grandma said, "Daisy, I have to do something. I've got to get my baby out of that nightmare."

The Chemist is her baby. Everyone was a baby once, even people in Club Fed.

Then she said, "Daisy, I'm afraid he's going to get hurt. He's not like them. He's a sweet boy. He wouldn't shoo a fly off a piece of watermelon."

After that visit, I was afraid, too.

* * *

The morning before the scary visit started like every third Sunday of the month. Grandma fixed me cheesy eggs. Then she styled my hair. French braids. She did my fingernails, too. Passion Purple, covered with a layer of glitter polish.

Then we hopped in her car with coffee for her and a disgusting vegetable juice for me. "Grandma," I said. "Don't you think it's weird there are houses across the street from the prison?"

"Those houses used to be across the street from the college admissions building. The prison came after the houses."

"They're nice houses, too. I wouldn't want to live there."

She pushed her cigarette through the crack in the window. "Hon, it's safer than your mom's trailer park. I'd bet good money on that."

"Grandma, it's a *mobile home* park. Trailers are for hauling. Besides, if she marries Alex, we'll probably move into his house."

"The boy toy owns a house?"

I groaned. "Gross! Stop calling him that."

"Does he have teeth?" Grandma played innocent, but I knew a dig when I heard it. Still, I laughed. Then I said, "Grandma, he's not so bad. He plays Monopoly and Uno with me. He came to my school concert, and I think he actually liked it. He said I sang the loudest."

Grandma took out a second cigarette. That means she's upset. "Does he really own a house?"

"He rents one half of the house to his brother and he lives in the other half. It's a duplex."

Grandma wanted to know more; I could tell. But I didn't say anything else. The Chemist told me a long time ago to be careful about giving information about Mom to Grandma and information about Grandma to Mom. "Nothing worse than women at war," he said. Grandma blames Mom for the Chemist dropping out of college, but Mom says he failed his way out of there. Then Grandma says Mom's wrong, and Mom says Grandma's wrong. Sometimes I wish my ears would fall off.

"Where's the house?"

I shrugged. I'm not going to say on the corner of Fourth and Plum because then she'll ask, "Is it nice?" and I'll say, "It's okay," and then she'll ask, "How many bedrooms?" and I'll say, "Three on each side," and she'll ask "What color is it?" and "Does it have air-conditioning?" and "Does your mother spend the night there?" and "How much money does he make as the tire store manager?" and it will NEVER END. And then when I get home, Mom will ask what Grandma asked me and what I told her and what Grandma said after I told her the thing I told her.

I changed the subject. "Can I get a candy bar from the machine when we get there?"

"You're going to get a big belly. That's where carbs go. Belly fat," she said. "But I guess I can spring for a candy bar."

"I had eggs for breakfast!"

"You're a pretty girl, but you've got roly-poly in your mom's side of the family. You're going to have to watch what you eat."

Grandma can talk for hours about working out and low-carb diets. She likes to point out she's in better shape than Mom. The Chemist always says Grandma's happiness is directly related to Mom's weight.

* * *

Grandma drove into the visiting center parking lot. I studied the tall fence that surrounds Club Fed. "Do you think it's electric? Like if we touched the fence, would we get electrocuted?"

"God no. It's not Alcatraz."

"What's Alcatraz?"

"It was a horrible prison for the worst of the worst. They put it on an island off California so nobody could ever escape."

"So nobody ever escaped Alcatraz?"

"Actually, they did. A couple of guys made it out. They were never found. It was such a big deal that Hollywood made a movie about it."

I made a mental note to rent that movie. "Think anyone ever escaped from Club Fed?"

She held my hand as we walked to the door. "I think about it every day."

That's what she said, and she hadn't even seen the Chemist's face yet.

* * *

On Sundays, the guard at the entrance was Aaron. His big belly made the buttons on his shirt stand at attention. If he laughs too hard, one of those buttons is going to pop and someone is going to lose an eye, and let me tell you, Aaron laughed a lot. He'd tell me I'm going to be as pretty as my mother someday; then he'd swoop his eyes at Grandma. She'd smile, run her fingers through her frosty, blond hair, and remind him I'm her grandbaby, and he'd act shocked. He always said, "I didn't know it was possible to be a grandmother at twenty-five!" And he laughed, and Grandma laughed, and I laughed because I thought he'd be nicer to the Chemist if I made him think he's funny.

We had to leave coats, purses, bags, and stuff in

a locker. We could bring money for the vending machine if it was in a clear sandwich bag.

Grandma told me if I had something lumpy in my pocket, Aaron would bring me to a special room and do a pat-down. At school, we'd call a guy like that a creeper, but at Club Fed, he's security.

After we cleared out our things, we walked through the metal detector and pushed through two heavy doors to the visiting center.

It was a big room with lots of windows, tables, and folding chairs. It used to be the student union, which means the student hangout. Against the wall were magazines, books, and board games. There were two Ping-Pong tables in the back. And kids. Lots of kids. I high-fived Derrick and Shane and Luci. I just waved at Juan-the-Nose-Picker. And I bent over and patted Calvin's head.

Then I saw him.

The Chemist waited at a small table by the window. At first I thought it was the sunlight hitting the glass, that somehow the bright light made the left side of his face look puffy and red and almost purple. Then he smiled. Only half of his lips moved. The other half was frozen.

Grandma sat down in a lump. "What the hell happened?"

"Looks way worse than it feels." The Chemist winked at me with his puffy brown eye, but the lid didn't quite close.

"Jacob? Really. What happened?"

"It was late, like midnight, and I got out of bed to take a leak and I walked into the wall!" He laughed. But it was a half laugh because his cheek was stiff.

Grandma's face went red. She slapped the table and said, "Stop with the crap. What happened?"

"Mom, it's nothing."

"Jacob Bauer. Tell me what happened."

"You know how we take classes? I accidentally welded my head. Clumsy, eh?" The Chemist smiled at me. I tried to smile back, but I couldn't make my face work.

"Jacob—"

"Mom! Let it chill, okay? No reason to worry the rug rat." He winked at me again. It was gross. His eyelids couldn't come together on account of their puffiness.

Grandma nudged me. "Daisy. Go find a magazine."

"I don't want a magazine."

"I want to talk to your father for a minute."

The Chemist stood up and gave me my first hug. You get two at Club Fed: one at hello and one at goodbye. But you can't linger because if you linger Aaron yells, "No lingering!"

"Daisy. Magazine. Now," Grandma said. "Be a good girl."

"But I want to talk to him, too!"

"Aurora Dawn Bauer! Go get a magazine from the rack. Find a long article and don't come back until you've read it twice. March!"

I marched. I picked a magazine with a sports car on the cover, held it nose level, and watched them.

The back of the Chemist's head was still, but Grandma's mouth moved like the wings of a hummingbird. Occasionally she'd slam her hands on the table or cross her arms. Then she started dabbing the corners of her eyes with her sleeves, and I could see mascara smudges. I marched right back.

"Daisy—" Grandma began, but I blurted out, "Eco-friendly sports cars!"

"What?"

"I read it twice. Eco-friendly! Sports cars!"

She sighed. "Hon, I'm not feeling so well. My stomach's all twisted up. We have to go soon."

"But I didn't even talk to him!"

The Chemist leaned forward and put his hand over my fist. "We have our Wednesday night phone date, right?"

Grandma stood up. "I'm going to the bathroom to fix my face. You two say goodbye." Off to the bathroom she went.

The Chemist pulled his hand away and crossed his arms just as Aaron called out, "No touching."

"I don't want to go yet," I said. "We just got here. Why's Grandma crying? And what happened to your face?"

"Baby, it's all good. Grandma's freaked out about nothing. It's how she gets. But you got no worries, okay?"

"What happened?" I tried to sound like my school principal, who I see when I forget my manners and talk back. She's Mrs. Tell-the-Truth-or-Else.

"Just a disagreement between gentlemen."

"You hit him back?"

"You don't think I'd just lay there and take it? Of course I hit them back. You should see their faces. Pepperoni pizza, baby."

"Them? More than one?"

"Hell, they were small. Like Muppets."

"Did you see a doctor?"

"It's Club Fed! Free medical care. Dental, too." His smile was swollen.

"Dental?"

He pointed in his mouth where a tooth was missing.

I gasped. "Does it hurt?"

"Truth?"

"Yes. Complete and total."

He shrugged. "Not much."

"How can you get hurt in Club Fed? There are guards! Are they napping or watching cartoons or what?"

"You ever see someone get bullied at school? You know, right under the eyes and ears of the teachers and janitors?" I nodded. That happens to Graham all the time. At recess Jesse Ellman yells, "Graham Cracker is a total slacker!" Sometimes he pushes Graham, too. That's when I pretend to be looking at the sky. So do the playground supervisors. I'd say something to Jesse, but I'm just a kid! The adults are supposed to take down the bullies. Plus Graham acts so stupid sometimes. If you don't want to be a bully magnet, then comb your hair and chew with your mouth closed and don't wear the same shirt three days in a row.

The Chemist said, "Club Fed's no different than school. It happens. But it's all good."

"It's not all good. It's bad!" I felt my chin shaking. This means I'm going to cry.

"Well, there is one bad thing." He leaned forward and whispered, "A terrible thing."

I was afraid to ask, but I did. "What?"

"The Tooth Fairy. She's not allowed in Club Fed. No special passes for fairies." He pretended to be all serious; then he laughed.

I rolled my eyes. "Right. Whatever."

"Can you smile for me? Please? It's my once-a-month Daisy smile. You know what I do with it?"

I shook my head and tried to hold my chin steady.

"I make a picture of you in my head. Your perfect face. Today it's gonna be your beautiful smile with your big brown eyes and those pretty braids Grandma put in your hair and your nails all done up. I memorize it all. Red sweatshirt. Little hoop earrings I gave you for Christmas." I touched my earrings. "I put that picture in my head and file it away. Then when I need to feel good about something, I pull it out and look at it. So smile for me, okay?"

I smiled. It was fake. It was lame. It was dumb. But it was for the Chemist.

Grandma put her hand on my shoulder. "Let's go, baby."

That's when I broke my first prison rule. I sat on the Chemist's lap and eased my cheek against his swollen one. And I gave him the tightest gentle squeeze I could. He was so skinny.

"It's fine, baby," he whispered. "I'm fine."

I didn't believe him. I didn't want to let him go. If I could just stay there, sitting on his lap, nobody would hurt him because they'd have to pry me off first. And nobody in Club Fed needs the extra trouble of pulling an almost twelve-year-old girl off her dad's lap.

"No extraneous touching and no lingering!" Aaron called.

Grandma patted my head. "Let's go, Daisy. We'll get fries and a shake today. Carbs be damned."

"No." I said it loud, but my face was buried in his shoulder. The Chemist gave me a squeeze and said, "We'll talk Wednesday, okay?"

"I want to know what happened."

"Daisy, you're super chill, but Grandma's a mess," he whispered. "She needs to get out of here. You take care of the old lady today. Go shopping. Hey, if you act cute, she'll probably buy you something. That'd be fun, huh?"

"No lingering!" Aaron's cheerful voice was less cheerful this time.

The Chemist put his hands up to show *he* wasn't the one lingering. I squeezed him tighter.

"Let's go," Grandma said.

"No!" I turned my face away from the Chemist and shouted at Grandma and Aaron. "I can hug my dad if I want! I'm not doing anything wrong. You can't stop me!"

Everyone was watching. Luci and the other kids shook their heads at me, and even Juan stopped picking his nose. Aaron pointed his finger and marched from the vending machine toward us.

27

"Daisy, if you don't release your father, I'm going to have to write you up. And that means you'll be banned from visiting for six months. You don't want that, do you?"

"This is not school!" Grandma hissed to me. "Here you have to listen!"

By now, everyone was watching, even the fedmates. The Chemist tried to push me off his lap, but I hung on tight. "Time to be a big girl," he said.

"No!"

"Daisy, this is your final warning." Aaron hovered over the Chemist, and there was no danger of his buttons popping off his shirt from jelly-belly laughter. "You've got me on the edge of a cliff, here. Don't push me over. Stand up now or I'll have to write a report."

So I stood up, to show I was listening, but I kept my arms around the Chemist, like my hands were glued to his back. Grandma pulled on me while the Chemist pushed. They were both telling me to stop and let go and listen and be good. As the Chemist talked to me, all I noticed was how half his face couldn't move. And the empty spot that had been home to a tooth.

I thought about how Mom kicked him out before I was old enough to have memories, how she yelled at him for money and called him deadbeat, how his own dad left and never took him out for mozzarella sticks, how a judge didn't care the explosion was a mistake, how fed-mates clobbered him for no reason, how the clerks at our visiting-day McDonald's stop knew to give Grandma extra napkins because she'd cry instead of eating a cheeseburger, hold the bun.

Aaron was going to give me the six-month visiting ban. I could see it in his mean eyes. Right then and there I decided to help the Chemist.

I pulled away from Grandma and the Chemist and climbed on the table. And I screamed, "If any of you creepers hurt my father, I will come after you! I will take a stick and poke out your eyeballs and play marbles with them! And I will fill your empty eye holes with . . . with . . . worms! And crickets! My dad shouldn't even be here! You're all mad because you're guilty and he's not!"

That's when the other security guards poured into the room.

DEAR JUDGE HENRY,

I'm supposed to say I'm sorry I linger-touched the Chemist and threatened those guys and their eyeballs. So, here you go: I'm sorry I linger-touched the Chemist and yelled about eyeballs and worms. Okay?

I am COOPERATING!

You know what happened next: I got the six-month visiting ban, and the prison people called the County, and the County sent a social worker to see me and my mom. He said the County could help me cope with my troubles by paying for counseling, but Mom said the County just wants in our business again. We'd had enough of the County.

After we got the papers for the visiting ban, Grandma and I drove back to her house. I couldn't erase what I'd done at the prison. But I wondered if the prison people might forgive me.

"Can you call the lawyer who gave me to you once a month? Maybe he can fix this mess."

She sniffled and said, "Please see if there's a napkin in the glove compartment." I found one, and she drove with one hand and blew her nose into the napkin. Then she said, "Daisy, I'm afraid he's going to get hurt, really hurt. He's not like them. He's a sweet boy."

"Either tell me what happened or stop talking about it." My chin was shaking again.

She sighed. "Some of the men there don't like him. Your father can be a smart talker, you know. He needs to learn to keep his mouth shut."

"That doesn't answer my question."

"They cornered him and beat him up."

"But why?"

"Because they're a bunch of thugs!"

"It's Club Fed." My voice turned into a yell. "You said killers and stranglers and stabbers don't go there! You said it's like getting a time out in your bedroom."

"It is. But it's also for people who committed drug crimes. And they're not always the nicest."

My heart flopped around because I'd been tricked. Grandma and Mom said he could take classes and work out and see movies on Friday nights. They left out the part about not-nice people and drugs.

Grandma squeezed my hand. "He's got you and he's got me. We're his family. We have to take care of him. I know that's what you were trying to do today. You were brave. It wasn't the smartest plan, honey, but it was brave. And I love you for it."

"You're not too mad?"

"No. Just incredibly sad. But we'll think of something, right?"

I squeezed her hand back. "We'll think of something."

* * *

So Grandma didn't exactly order me to break the Chemist out of prison. But she told me I was brave and that we had to take care of him. That translates, don't you think?

DEAR JUDGE HENRY,

I will tell you three things about Graham Hassler aka Graham Cracker.

Number one: He is a pain in my butt! Our moms have been friends since Graham and me went to the Head Start preschool. They've always wanted us to be buddies, too, but he drives me crazy, and we argue all the time. You know how when moms get together, they make jokes about their kids going to prom and getting married? Well, our moms joke about our future *divorce.*

Number two: Graham wanted to run away. He hates school. He hates wearing thrift-store jeans that don't cover his socks. He hates the extra hours his mom works on account of their electricity getting turned off. When we stood at the bus stop, if Graham wasn't talking about football or snakes or cowboys, he was always making plans to run away. Living in the mountains, by the ocean, or in Australia. Working as a samurai, singer, or horse trainer. He always had a new plot; always something better than here.

Number three: Graham is a pest to me, but he's a big chicken with everyone else. He puts stuff in my desk like wrinkled carrots and spitballs and even stinky socks! Then he laughs and laughs. But he *hides* from Jesse Ellman, the jerk who yells, "Hey Graham Cracker, you forget your deodorant today? Cuz you smell like trash. Oh, wait, you *are* trash!" Graham should kick him in the shins; that's what I'd do.

Security Guard Aaron says I pushed him over a cliff, and that's why he gave me the visiting ban. Well, I got pushed over a cliff, too. You could say Aaron took me to the cliff when he banned me from visiting for six months, and Grandma walked me toward the edge when she told me to help the Chemist. But Graham pushed me. Don't yell about taking responsibility until you hear the whole thing. You'll see.

* * *

The next week, I was sitting on a swing at the River Estates playground, which is no playground. The slide is metal. It soaks the sun and burns your legs in the summer. You scoot fast at the top, but you slam to a stop because the bottom is sticky. I scrubbed that spot with soapy water, and it's still sticky. There's also a teeter-totter that gives me splinters, three swings that creak and moan, and a sandbox without any sand. I refuse to say playground. I call it a play dump.

It's like calling the prison Club Fed. Giving something bad a nice name or a funny name doesn't change it. *Defecate* is a fancy word for poop—the Chemist told me that—but it doesn't cover up the stink. Take River Estates Mobile Home Park as an example. To me, *estates* says a neighborhood with brick houses that have shiny grills on the decks and people who take down their Christmas lights before June. But it's not. The places here are saggy and rusty and embarrassed. There isn't even a *river* by River Estates Mobile Home Park!

There I was, swinging and waiting for Mom to finish work. I heard a door slam behind me, and a few seconds later Graham was on the swing next to me singsonging, "I know something you don't know!"

I pumped my legs faster and ignored him. Why did his trailer have to be next to the play dump? I couldn't get a second alone on that swing.

"I know something you don't know." He was louder and more sing-y. "And it's about yoooo-ouuuu. So do you wanna know? Do you?"

"I don't care." If I acted like I wanted to know, he would stretch it out forever.

"Do you wanna know?"

"Not really. But whatever."

Graham pumped his legs to keep up with me.

For a moment there was nothing but the sounds of the swings creak-squeaking. Then he said, "You're going to stay with us for a week because your mom's going on vacation!"

I made stiff legs and dug my feet into the ground. My swing groaned and stopped. "What?"

"Your mom asked my mom if we'd watch you for a week. Alex is taking her to a resort in Mexico. I guess they want some kissing time." He made lip smooches. "And you don't get to go."

"You better be wrong!" I shouted.

Alex is ancient. He's at least forty, and he's got a little ring of black-and-gray hair around his head. He's been dating Mom for a year. Her other boyfriends treated me like a pest. Mom always said I'm more important than men, but that was bull. She'd hang on them, they'd both ignore me, and then Mom would send me to bed early.

But Alex is different. He calls me his buddy. Alex doesn't have kids, so he said he's counting on me to teach him how to be cool, which is our joke. So why wouldn't they take me on vacation, too? His buddy? Mom's more-important kid? Hah.

"Hey, don't blame me. Blame your mom and her stupid boyfriend. I'd be pissed off, too. I'd run away to the resort and get a job as a surfing instructor."

"You don't know how to surf."

"Duh. I have to learn first."

"You probably got it wrong. You never listen, Graham Cracker!"

He stopped swinging and kicked dirt at me. "I listen. I'm not deaf, you know."

Graham started talking about horses and snakes. My head burned. Mom on vacation without me! To a beach! She never went swimming with *me* because she said her legs look like sausages. I guess Alex likes sausage! Come to think of it, they go to the stadium theater without me on account of the R ratings. They probably pick R-rated movies so I *can't* go. And Mom always asks Alex what he wants for supper. Chili. Lasagna. Italian beef.

Doesn't matter—she'll stay by the stove until it's done. But me? She just slaps fish sticks on the table whether I want them or not.

Fish sticks, Judge Henry, fish sticks! They must always be on sale.

DEAR JUDGE HENRY,

Sure enough, Mom told me Alex was taking her on a trip because they needed some "alone time." I wanted to tell her I was alone all the time and it wasn't so great. I wanted to ask her what would happen if their alone time was amazingly fabulous and they stayed in Mexico. Would Mom ask the County to take me? A long time ago, the County threatened to put me in a foster home, which is a place for kids when their parents need parents. But Mom got her act together. She started going to the alcohol meetings with Kari, and Kari became her sponsor. That means Kari is the parent of Mom not drinking anymore.

Then Mom got a job at the nursing home, and in the fall, she's going to school to be a real nurse and I get a trampoline from her first paycheck. I reminded her that River Estates bans trampolines because they probably hate fun. Alex smiled all big and said, "Hey, buddy, there's no ban on trampolines at my house."

Buddy? Whatever.

I didn't act sad or mad or anything when Mom told me about the trip. I said, "Whatever." And she said, "Is that your new favorite word?"

I shrugged and turned on the TV.

"You need a positive attitude," Mom said. "You're acting like a teenager and you're not even twelve! Can't you be happy for me?"

"Whatever."

"You know, I'd like to talk to you, but talking involves two people actually talking. Not just shrugging and eye-rolling and whatever-ing."

"Why can't I stay with Grandma? Why Graham Cracker?" The question was a waste of time, but I asked just to see Mom's face crinkle up. That's how mad I was.

"Use his real name, Daisy."

"Why do I have to stay with Graham *Hassler* instead of Grandma?"

"Because she lives thirty minutes away, and

there aren't any kids by her town house for you to play with."

"So? Kari works all day. It's spring break. We're gonna be home all day with nothing to do."

"You're staying with Kari because she's my best friend, and it's easy. If you need anything from home, all you have to do is walk fifty feet. If you need any help while Kari's working, Mrs. Mundez is six trailers away. She's a sweetheart," Mom said. Then she acted like she just thought of the best reason ever. "And you'll have someone to play with!"

"Great. A whole week with Graham."

She was still yackity-yacking when I grabbed the remote and turned up the volume. Mom sighed and texted something on her phone. Probably to Alex. Probably something like, *Can't wait to be alone!*

And me with Graham for a week. A person could go crazy in a week, you know.

DEAR JUDGE HENRY,

Everything fell apart the day Mom and Alex left.

Graham and I were on spring break, so we had to hang out at his place *all day*. With nothing to do. Nothing! His mom told us to watch movies and make a frozen pizza for lunch while she worked, but Graham can never sit through an entire movie.

"You wanna go outside?" he asked every fifteen minutes. His bangs were greasy and hanging past his eyes. He'd brush them aside, and they'd fall into his eyelashes again.

"It was rainy and cold the first time you asked, and it's still rainy and cold," I said. "I could cut your bangs."

"Remember when we used to play horse race and I'd always win?" He looked so proud of himself.

"Remember when we used to play arm

wrestling and I'd always win?" That shut him up for about ten minutes. Then he said, "Whatcha want to do?"

"My grandma's a stylist so I'm naturally good at hair cutting." This sounded like a good idea. His hair was shaggy and gross, and I'd been thinking I could go to beauty school and open a shop with Grandma. She could work on the old people, and I'd work on the young people. We'd be both hip *and* classic and make a fortune.

"I'm bored. Why are you just sitting around?" Graham stood on the couch and bounced. "I wanna go outside or play a game. Mom won't let me use the computer when she's not here because she's afraid I'll give it a virus. But we could guess her password. Wanna guess her password? I bet it's Maggie. That was her first dog. Half the people in the world use their pet's name for a password."

I crossed my arms and said, "You need your bangs cut."

"My mom wouldn't like it." He jumped to the

floor and dug around in his pocket. "I'm going to show you something that my uncle gave me. It's super cool. And I don't tell people about it, but because we're trapped for a whole week, we're going to need it."

Graham opened his fist and showed me an old penny.

"So what?" I said. "You can't buy anything with a penny."

"It's not just a plain old penny. Look at the date on it—1919. It's old. Really, really old!"

"So?"

He pushed his bangs back and sighed. "It's so old it's become an Idea Coin. You know my uncle who lives in Michigan? Well, he gave this coin to me when we went to see him. My uncle said an old coin with the same numbers—like this, with a nineteen and a nineteen—gets special powers because they've been in so many pockets and purses. It's picked up the idea energy from thousands of people over a hundred years. Hold it in your hand, squeeze it real tight against your head, and a cool idea will come to you."

"Your uncle told you that?"

"Yup."

"Were you bugging him about being bored?"

"Daisy, it works! Every time I use it I get the coolest ideas. Remember when we had that blizzard and I got you outside and we made an igloo and it was super cool? Even you said it was the best snow day ever. Well, the Idea Coin told me to knock on your door that day."

"You sure it wasn't your mom?" Graham believes everything. Once Abbey Harris told him she'd be his friend for a whole week if he gave her five dollars. I warned him she was full of it, but he didn't listen. He stole five dollars from his mom's wallet and gave it to Abbey. She ran off with the money and told her friends and they all laughed at him.

"Nope. It was the coin. You just can't overuse it because it drains the idea energy. Don't use it to decide between playing a video game and watching a movie. Save it for desperate times. And I think this is a desperate time. Here, put it in your hand."

I took the penny from his fist.

"Squeeze it tight. You're right-handed, right?"

"Yeah."

"Okay. Keep it in your right hand. Now close your eyes. And breathe deep. Are your eyes closed?"

"They're closed."

"Are you squeezing it tight?"

"I'm squeezing it tight."

"Okay. Now don't open your eyes. Slowly lift your right hand and hold it against your forehead."

"It's against my forehead."

"Not your fist," he said. "Press the actual penny against your actual forehead and hold it there."

"Fine."

"Now the Idea Coin will soak into your brain. Give it some time. Just open your mind." He was so close I could smell his cereal breath. "Okay, Daisy. Tell me the idea."

I didn't give it any soaking time. I blurted out, "I should cut your bangs!"

* * *

Ten minutes later, half of Graham's hair was *gone*. It happened so fast. I did it just like Grandma. We were in the bathroom, and I held a chunk of hair between two fingers and snip, snip, snip. I used scissors from a kitchen drawer. Like the living room floor in our trailer, his bangs went up and down and back up, a tiny hair roller coaster, so I had to cut more to fix it. Then the bangs were too short and the rest of his hair was hanging down his neck like strings of spaghetti, so I trimmed that up, too. I figured shorter hair would bring out the blue in his eyes. But it wasn't level, either, so I had to keep cutting.

"Maybe I should call my grandma." I put the scissors on the sink and tried combing the tuffs of hair into a smooth cap of blondness. "Is your mom going to be mad?"

He shrugged. "The Idea Coin is never wrong! Besides, I don't care. It's kinda cool."

"But will she be mad?"

"Yup. She'll freak." He turned his head from side to side and squinted his eyes. "I look like I'm in a rock band. I should play guitar or drums. Or tuba! You can use a tuba to make fart sounds. Did you know that?"

I begged Graham to wear a baseball cap for a week, until my mom got home, and he promised he would.

* * *

At five o'clock, Kari pushed the door open with her hip and stepped inside. The cool spring air came in with her. In one hand, she had a takeout pizza. In the other was her cell phone, pressed against her ear. "Just let me get the kids settled, okay? I know. I know. I'll call you right back."

She put the phone in her purse and pulled two

plates from the cupboard. She didn't even blink at Graham's baseball cap. "I've got a bunch of stuff that just exploded. So here's dinner. I need you two to stay out of trouble. I'm going out for a while."

Graham frowned. "Where are you going?"

"Out."

My stomach rumbled when she opened the pizza box. Large pepperoni. We'd had frozen pepperoni pizza at lunch, but you can never have too much pepperoni pizza. I could eat it every meal of every day.

"Why? It's Monday night." Graham sat down at the table while Kari poured two glasses of milk and put plates in front of us.

"Because." Her eyes looked red, like maybe she'd been crying. She wasn't wearing her uniform, so she had stopped somewhere and changed.

Graham crossed his arms and stared at her. "*Because* is not an answer!"

"I don't have to explain. It involves adult stuff, okay? I just need you two to take care of yourselves and stay out of trouble. You can watch a movie. Brush your teeth and hit the pillows by ten."

"But there's no school tomorrow."

"I'll be home about ten, and your butts better be in bed. Mrs. Mundez is home if you need her, or you can call my cell."

Then she patted my shoulder, kissed the top of Graham's baseball cap, and closed the door behind her.

I grabbed a slice and chowed. Graham stared at the table.

"What's wrong? I thought you were hungry."

One by one, he picked off the pepperonis and ate them.

"What's wrong?" I asked again.

Graham said, "She had that voice."

I closed my eyes and replayed the last few minutes in my mind. He was right. "Yeah, she did. You think it was the broke-up-with-the-boyfriend voice? Or the-car-needs-a-new-engine voice?"

"Not sure. Maybe the lost-my-job voice."

"Ohhhhh, that's baaaaaad," I said. "Then you'll have to get money for bills from the County."

Graham agreed. "That's the worst."

"Was it her drinking voice?"

Graham poured his milk in the sink, rinsed the glass, and filled it with water. He gulped it down. "I don't like milk. I'd rather have water or berry bonanza juice. Wanna play Crazy Eights?"

This time I didn't repeat the question. I actually felt bad for old Graham Cracker. So I said sure, and I won four hands in a row.

DEAR JUDGE HENRY,

That night, I had a horrible dream. The Chemist was walking through a long hall and two people jumped him and started pounding on him. I ran and yelled the weirdest thing. "Crickets in your eye holes!" The jumpers turned around. It was my mom and Alex. I jumped on Alex's back and pulled at his ring of hair. Mom kept pounding on the Chemist until there was nothing but a wrinkled orange uniform, like a towel tossed to the floor after a shower.

"What'd you do?" I screamed at her.

"He'll be back in time for your high school graduation." She crossed her arms. "And you, little Miss Dawn Dawn! What did *you* do?"

"Huh?"

"To Alex! What did you do to Alex?"

I looked down and realized I'd turned Alex into a turkey. Mom screamed, "Alex!" while I screamed, "Daddy!"

Graham shook me awake. "You were having a bad dream."

I sat up and breathed in and out. Deep and calm.

"Man, your breath smells like pee and rot!" He scooted away and plugged his nose.

"Shut up, Graham!"

"Pee and rot and toe slime." He pretended to slide off the bed and pass out on the floor.

I threw my pillow on his face. "Jerk."

He didn't move, and I didn't move. I pulled up the sheet and wrapped it around me. The wind was blowing hard. I could hear the swings creaking and squeaking from the play dump. Far away, a dog barked.

Graham sat up and balanced the pillow on his head. "My mom's not home."

"What time is it?"

"I bet if I told a creepy story I could make you scared."

"What time is it? Simple question!"

"Midnight."

We sat in the dark for a few minutes, Graham balancing the pillow on his head and me tracing the edge of the sheet with my pinky.

"Let's go to the play dump," Graham said.

"Okay."

I changed into my jeans and a sweatshirt, and pulled on my spring coat. I looked through the bathroom window. The moon lit the River Estates Mobile Home Park almost as good as if the security lights were working. The spot where Kari parked her car was empty. It seemed like her parking spot was always empty.

* * *

Graham and I stood on the swings and clutched the chains. It didn't take much motion from us to get them swinging. The wind was howling. We could see the park's entrance through the trailers to our right and Graham's place was straight ahead. It would be a quick dodge inside once we noticed headlights.

"You know, this isn't the kind of babysitting my mom was planning," I said.

"Do you think Frank the Creeper is awake? His lights are on." Frank had long biker hair and gray eyes and a cobra tattooed on his arm. He never said "Hello" or "Hey, there" or "What's up." He just gave a little head lift when he saw someone, and he turned away and spit tobacco juice. Frank the Creeper was disgusting.

"Should we call your mom's cell?"

"You were saying something about a turkey when you were dreaming. What the heck kind of nightmare was that?"

He was trying to swing faster than me, so I pulled hard on the chains to speed up. I said, "I don't remember. Dreams don't make sense."

"I bet I could tell you a story about a ghost turkey and make you scared."

"I bet I could tell you a story about Frank the Creeper and make you scared."

"Bet you couldn't."

"Should we call your mom's cell?"

Graham let go of the swing and leaped into the air, landing on his feet. Then the swing hit him in the butt. He pretended it knocked him over, and he rolled through the dirt and onto the weed patch.

"Ouch," he said. "There's a thistle in here."

"Graham! Should we call Kari's cell? Or should we call my mom's cell? Or somebody's cell?"

Graham picked weeds from his hair. He held up a dandelion. "I used to think this was a daisy until you showed me that picture."

"Dandelions are weeds. Daisies are flowers. I wouldn't name myself after a weed!"

"I wanna new name, too," he said. "Like Long-dragon. Or Roger. When I move to Canada, I'm going to call myself Roger F. Longdragon. The *F* will be for Ford."

I jumped off the swing, landed on my feet, and then did a ballet spin to get out of the swing's way. I dropped on the ground next to him, sat with folded legs, and loud-whispered, "Graham. This is me screaming, but I can't scream because people are sleeping. So pretend I'm screaming. Should we call my mom or my grandma or your mom? Now answer me or I'll scream. And Frank the Creeper will wake up." I made an evil but quiet laugh. "And he'll chop us into pieces . . . and eat us!"

Graham popped the top off the dandelion and threw it at me. It hit me near my eye.

"Nice," I said.

"You're welcome."

"Graham! Answer me!"

"Jeez. I don't know. Why should I know?"

"She's *your* mom. That's why."

"Here's the way I see it. We could call my mom. But we both know she's at the Rattlesnake and can't remember where she dropped her phone. We could call your mom. But we both know she's slobbering on Alex and they've got their phones turned off for their slobber time. We could call your grandma, but she'd freak and call the County."

"Oh."

"That's why I'm running away soon."

I sighed. "When's the big move?"

"I should've left already. I'd be a horse trainer by now. Or maybe a forklift driver."

"Where this time?"

"To Canada," he said. Graham sat up and threw a rock at his trailer. The bang echoed in the night. "I'm pissed at my mom. Extra pissed because I bet she got fired. She called in sick three times last week so she could hang out with that guy she met. Ryan? Brian? Something like that."

"I'm pissed at my mom, too," I said. "But why Canada?"

"Because I want to live in a cabin and learn how to hunt and fish. I'll grow carrots because that's the only vegetable I like. I'm not going to school because I never learn anything anyway. I'm going to climb trees and make my own flour and ride a huge horse through the forest. I'll eat cinnamon bread with honey on it every day."

"What's wrong with being an American farmer?"

"Because I'll be an outlaw. When you run away,

you're an outlaw. And it's easy for outlaws to hide in Canada. There's so many trees. Millions. The police don't go into the woods on account of the grizzly bears."

"So you want to take your chances with grizzly bears?"

"I'm going to train them." He sighed, like I was stupid. "And just in case, I'll have a gun. I'll need one for hunting anyway."

"You like hamBEARger?" Hilarious! I laughed my tail off.

"Ha-ha. You're funny as a math test." He rubbed his very short hair.

I said, "Cabins don't have water and stuff we're used to. If cabins had those things, they'd be called houses."

"Look around, Daisy. These are just rusty metal cabins."

I pointed at his place. "Your rusty cabin has a microwave and a dishwasher and Internet! And lights. Lights are important."

"Haven't you heard of *solar power*? I will build

some panels for the cabin and use the sun for electricity. Boom. Done."

I pulled three long weeds and started to braid them. My butt was cold, but I liked the night air and the wind. I felt more awake than during the day.

"You should come, Daisy."

"No thanks."

"You really want to live with Alex and watch him slobber-kiss your mom? And go to our stupid school where everyone's stupid? And play in this play dump? And live in a town where parents go to the Rattlesnake Bar and Grill and act like beer zombies?"

"The Rattlesnake has the best mozzarella sticks." My stomach started to clench like a fist.

"Hah. Wait until you find out *your* mom is hanging out there again. It'll happen."

"My mom doesn't drink!"

He laughed all crazy and rolled around in the grass. "Duh! That's the point! Neither does mine.

It's called *drinking again*." He threw another dandelion at me. "And guess what? Canada is one of only three countries in the world where alcohol is illegal."

"Really?" I squinted. "How would you know?"

"I read! Sometimes Mom brings home the newspaper from the break room at work."

"Doesn't matter. I have to see the Chemist."

"You can't see him for six months! That's like forever!"

"Aaron, the main guard, cut the ban to three months," I said. "I think he likes my grandma."

"There's only one time when three months isn't an eternity. Summer!"

My chin was shaking. I felt a little sweaty, and the wind turned my sweat cold. I shivered. My stomach hurt from the nightmare and all of Graham's yackity-yack Canada and yackity-yack Rattlesnake Bar and Grill.

Graham stood up. He had a couple more rocks, and he threw them one at a time at the play dump sign. Every time he missed, he stepped closer. I figured he'd have to be a foot away from the sign to actually hit it.

Then something flashed in the weeds where Graham had been sitting. Just a glimmer. I crawled on my hands and knees and saw the glimmer again. I rubbed my hands on the ground until I felt a penny. I squeezed it in my fist and held my hand to where the moonlight shined just so. I squinted and read the numbers. "Nineteen nineteen." The Idea Coin had rolled out of Graham's pocket.

Then, Judge Henry, my stomach clenched again—so hard that I pressed one hand over my belly and the hand with the Idea Coin against my head. It was like cold water pouring over my body. I shivered. I wrapped both my arms around myself and tried to squeeze away the cold. The coin didn't come off with my hand. I could feel it stuck to my forehead.

The cold turned to a wave of heat. The warmth pressed through me, and all I could hear was the wind and the TV from Frank the Creeper's trailer.

And that's when the idea shot out of the coin and into my brain. The Chemist. Me. Canada. Graham. Trees. Carrots. Cinnamon bread with honey.

The shivering stopped. The fist in my stomach unclenched.

"What's that on your head?" Graham asked as he walked away from the play dump sign.

"The Idea Coin," I whispered.

He quickly kneeled next to me. "What'd it say?"

I pulled it off my forehead and licked it so it would stick to his forehead, too. I pressed it where his bangs used to be and stared into his eyes.

Then the words came out.

"We're breaking the Chemist out of prison and going to Canada!"

It's all blurry now. I honestly can't say if he said it or if I said it or if we said it together at the exact same time, but looking back, I think that voice and those words echoed down from the moon.

THE SECOND PART

DEAR JUDGE HENRY,

You need a lot of things for a prison break and a new life in a cabin in Canada. Like a cabin. And a car and money and food and solar panels for electricity and Internet. The next day we made lists and counted money. I had forty dollars in birthday money, and we counted sixty-five dollars in Mom's change jar. Graham had seven dollars and fifty cents.

As for Kari, she came home after we fell asleep that night. At breakfast she told us the printing press cut her job. Not enough orders for wedding invitations and business cards. She looked upset, and she cursed the Internet, but she was sober. We could tell because her eyes weren't half closed and she didn't smell like perfume cover-up and she wasn't taking aspirin.

"Mom, did you get fired?"

Kari yelled, "You are not the parent, Graham! I'm the parent."

"Jeez, I didn't even swear. Just a simple question. Because you promised this time you wouldn't cause problems at your job." Graham's arms were crossed, like he was going to ground her or something.

Kari acted like she hadn't heard him. "I won't be home for a few nights. I have to look at job listings at the County Center for Unskilled and Underskilled Workers." She lit a cigarette when she said "County" and acted like she didn't care about the unskilled and underskilled parts.

I said, "You're not unskilled! You're a sponsor at those meetings to stop drinking. You're smart. That thing where you eat all your food at a restaurant and then complain about how bad it was so you don't have to pay? Brilliant! You have more uses for duct tape than anyone. Fixing sleds. Keeping your rearview mirror on your car. Hanging up pictures."

Graham mumbled, "Maybe there's a job for her in the taping factory."

I was only trying to help her see the positive side.

* * *

After Kari left, Graham and I started a planning notebook.

The first pages were lists of things we needed immediately (food, car, clothes, money, etc.) and things we'd need later (solar panels, canned food, hunting rifle, carrot seeds, etc.). Then came our new identities, Roger Ford Longdragon and Anastacia Katherine-Elise Trenton, along with suggested hairstyles, hair colors, and colored eye contacts. I pasted pictures from Kari's magazines of people we could look like.

Graham laughed. "Right. That's *exactly* like you. A twenty-one-year-old model with . . ." He pointed at her chest.

"Shut up! You are so gross." I was never sleeping in the same bedroom with him again, even if there were two beds and a moat filled with crocodiles between us.

"And this fat kid is supposed to be me?" He slapped me with the notebook. "Fat-tastic. Thanks."

"He was in an ad for allergy medicine. Find your own disguise, Roger F. Longdragon. Get back to business."

I opened the notebook to the map section. I'd sketched the Club Fed buildings from memory. I'd marked where the fed-mates ate and smoked.

"This can't be too hard. It's only a low-security prison. But we need more detail," Graham said. "Where do the guards stand? Where do the fed-mates walk?"

"I don't know much about the guards. Just Aaron because he seems to be in charge. He's kind of fat and not very fast. Anyone could outrun him," I said.

"Even you?" Graham poked me.

"Knock it off. We're working here. So the buildings . . . hmm . . . I don't know what all of them are used for. One is a gym and three are for sleeping and there's a cafeteria. Across the street are houses. It's basically in a neighborhood."

Graham rubbed his chin. "That's going to make it hard, huh?"

"Well, there's nothing weird about two kids hanging out in a neighborhood."

"True," he said. "We should stay away from the visiting center after what you did. Your face is probably on a wanted poster."

"Very funny."

"I thought so." His smile was big and geeky. "Where'd you say they stand around and smoke?"

I pointed to an area of the lawn right by the cafeteria, where the grass slopes into a gentle hill and the hill goes flat before the fence line. There's grass on both sides of the fence. Grass on the one side for the fed-mates, and grass and a sidewalk on the other side for the neighbors. "The Chemist talks about smoking after dinner, and dinner is at five, so I'd guess they stand here, right outside the cafeteria exit, until about five-thirty."

"How tall is this fence? Can he jump it?"

I was thinking about how it could work when Graham started talking. "That's where we'll nab him, right at the fence, right during the smoke break. We'll get the car as close as possible. Then we'll signal him or something. I'll create a distraction to buy time so the guards don't notice right away. I'll . . . I'll pretend to have a seizure in the street or . . . well, the seizure thing's good, huh? Really good. Then the Chemist will jump the fence, and we'll race away in the car. Back roads all the way to Canada."

"Car? What car? And the fence has razor wire at the top!"

"What's razor wire?"

"It's like a huge Slinky on top of the fence. The wire is so sharp it'll slice your hands right off!"

"How are we gonna get around the razor stuff?"

"How are we going to get around the not-having-a-car stuff?"

We both sat there, our chins on our hands, looking at the notebook. I said, "If we had wire cutters, we could throw them over the fence for the

Chemist. He could climb and cut the razor wire. Then it'd be safe for him to jump."

"With wire cutters, we could cut a hole in the fence!"

"I don't think so. After Grandma told me the fence wasn't electric, I touched it. The razor wires on top look really thin, but the fence is like . . . it would be like cutting through really thick stuff."

Graham slammed his chair into the table. Like a soldier, he announced. "Fetching wire cutters!"

And he left. I shouted out the door, "What about the car?" Graham rounded the corner past Mrs. Mundez. Frank the Creeper was working on his motorcycle. He looked at me. I looked at him, but I was afraid to say "Hello" or "How the heck are ya" or anything. He spit tobacco juice, and I slammed the door.

* * *

Twenty minutes later, Graham came back with wire cutters, a dirty face, and a braggy smile. "I broke into the maintenance shed."

"Really?!"

"In the back of the shed, there's this huge plank falling off and it's all wet and covered in mold. Well, I kicked three times and I got a hole big enough to climb through. Ripped my pants. But I found the wire cutters on the shelf with a bunch of other crap they don't use around here."

I took them from his hands. "Wow. They're heavy!"

"Change in plans." Graham lifted his sweaty arms and kissed his muscles. "You'll be the guard and fed-mate distraction, and I'll be the wire-cutter thrower."

I laughed. "Right. You're soooo strong. But soooo stupid. The Chemist hasn't seen you in ages. If he sees this boy throwing something at the fence, he'll be like, 'What's up with that weird dude?' But if it's me, he'll run right down there."

Graham wanted to be the wire-cutter thrower. I could tell. "Hey," I said. "How about you help me practice?"

"Sure. You'll need a coach."

Sometimes Graham acted like such a big shot. I said, "I don't *need* a coach."

"Fine. I'll be your trainer."

"I don't *need* a trainer."

"What am I supposed to do then?"

"Watch and learn."

* * *

Turns out, I needed a coach, a trainer, and a fetcher. After lunch, Graham and I walked a half mile down the county road near the woods. I had to guess the height of the fence. We looked for a tree branch that seemed the right height, and I threw the wire cutters straight in the air, hoping they'd go higher than the branch. But those cutter things zoomed straight down. We screamed and jumped into the ditch.

"You almost killed us!"

I crouched in the weeds, shaking. "That throw was just my guesstimate. Let's try it again."

"You can't throw it straight above your head. It has to go *over* the fence. *Over*." Graham made a half circle with his arm.

So I threw it high and over. And that stupid tree branch got in the way and caught it.

"Oops."

Graham glared at me.

I tried to stay perky. "Can you climb a tree?"

"Not that one."

We searched the ditch for sticks and rocks and threw them at the cutters so the tree would loosen its grip. Nothing worked. Graham said, "Wait here."

About twenty minutes later, he came back pushing a wheelbarrow. It was full of old paint cans, a small radio, a couple hunks of wood, three boots, part of a shovel, a baseball, and a bat.

"Where'd you get this stuff?"

"I used a hammer to break a bigger hole in the maintenance shed. That's where I got the wheelbarrow. Then I dug through the Dumpster and found stuff heavy enough to hit the wire cutters and knock 'em down."

"So why so much stuff? All we need is one or two heavy things."

Graham scratched his head. "Oh yeah."

"You should have told *me* your plan and I could've saved you from Dumpster diving. You smell like . . . chicken fat and dog turds!" Which couldn't be true because nobody in River Estates picks up their dogs' turds.

"Well, you smell like chicken fat and dog turds and you haven't even been in a Dumpster!"

I quit talking. He'd never stop coming up with stink-names, because in that game he is a champ, and we had to get those cutters down.

Graham threw the paint cans and missed the branch entirely. I hit the branch's edge with the small radio, and the radio swung from the tree by its cord. "Outstanding work," Graham said. "Now we got two things stuck up there."

The ball and boots failed, too. I took the baseball bat, swung it high in the sky and *wham*! The bat *and* cutters came down.

I practiced the wire-cutter throw for almost an

hour, until I could throw a high arc that cleared the tree. My arms ached. "I think we've had enough practice for today."

On the way back to Graham's trailer, we took turns pushing each other in the wheelbarrow. I was sure nobody would notice. I'm not sure River Estates even had a maintenance man. We put it back in the shed, and Graham used a hammer to close up the big hole.

We brushed the dirt and grass off our jeans before going inside, where we slammed big glasses of water. Spring wasn't just warm like usual. Hot. It was July hot. Then I remembered the most important part of the plan. Wheels, and not the wheelbarrow kind. The car kind.

"Graham," I gasped from drinking so fast. "You said we'd have a car and a driver."

He belly-flopped on the couch. "The car is a 1996 Oldsmobile. Dark blue. The perfect get-away color. Perfect for back roads. We'll hide in the day and drive at night so it'll be hard to see us."

"Key problem. We don't know how to drive!"

He took the planning notebook and wrote, *The Graham Cracker Plot*. "Sounds cool, you think?"

"What about the Daisy . . . Flower . . . Pot?"

He exploded into giggles, and I had to admit it sounded pretty stupid. When he finally stopped laughing he said, "Let's make some sandwiches and hide them in the fridge drawer with the bag of wrinkled carrots. Mom doesn't go in that drawer. Then we'll have food for a couple days."

He was making me crazy, and we weren't even at the cabin. I pulled the notebook out of his hands.

"Key problem!" I repeated. "We don't know how to *drive*."

Graham looked really proud of himself. "We don't. But Mom's cousin Ashley does. And she's got a car."

Hmm, I thought. *Hmm*.

DEAR JUDGE HENRY,

I will tell you three things about Ashley.

Number one: She is twenty-four and pretty, with bright blue eyes and a smile from a teeth-whitening commercial. She wears hats and wigs and scarves to hide the marks on her head.

Number two: The marks on her head came from an accident with a semi. Her parents died, and Ashley's brain crisscrossed. After the accident, a lawyer zoomed to court. The truck company paid Ashley money, but half went to the lawyer. Half! Then Ashley's brother said he'd take care of her and her money in California. Good for him because becoming an actor pays way less than being a lawyer. Bad for Ashley because when he sent

her back to Minnesota, he had a fancy sports
car and she had suitcases patched with duct
tape. The County said Ashley couldn't move
to Graham's place on account of his mom
having two bedrooms and her own problems.
So Ashley moved to a County apartment
where people come by to help her pay bills
and make her clean the house and stuff.

Number three: Ashley's moods change a lot. I
think she has an alarm clock in her body that
says, "Noon. Time to giggle! Three o'clock.
Crabby time! Ten o'clock. Be sad and stop
talking to people!"

Now that's one looooong and sad story. Mom
tells it to *everybody* with gasps and f-bombs.
The Chemist says it's creepy to talk about Ashley
like she's a reality TV star. Mom's fascinated, the
Chemist says, because it makes her feel better
about her own crappy life.

* * *

The next morning, after Kari left for work, I stuffed our backpacks while Graham used a highlighter to trace the back roads on a road map. We had to walk to Ashley's.

I asked, "You sure Ashley will help?"

"I told you a hundred times what my mom says. Ashley was the queen of adventure even before the accident."

I hoped he was right, because Plan B was taking my mom's car and driving it ourselves. Graham said he was plenty experienced from his go-cart riding. But cars are bigger, and they don't go around in circles. Sometimes cars hit trucks, and when that happens, drivers turn into Ashley.

"Oh my God, it's heavy!" Graham groaned as he lifted his pack. He leaned against the stove, which Kari apparently never cleaned. The stove was covered with crumbs, charred pieces of stuff that had been food, and sticky spots. "What's in this backpack?"

"Mom's change jar. And the notebook and the wire cutters from the shed."

He squinted at me. "What are you carrying?"

"Sandwiches and your mom's sweat suit so the Chemist has something to wear. I didn't have room for hardly any of my own clothes. We'll have to get stuff in Canada."

"That's all?"

I looked away. "A book. Two rolls of toilet paper because you just never know. Some pictures. No big deal."

"Pictures?"

"Yeah. So what?" My chin felt shaky, but just for a minute. He didn't notice. I forced myself to think forward, not backward. "Graham, the most important thing is in your pocket. That's not good. Let me carry it in my backpack."

He pulled out the Idea Coin and held it in the light from the window, studying it closely. "No way. It's mine. I keep it."

"You would have lost it the other night in the weeds! It's too important for pockets."

"Why? You got a safe in the backpack? No way. It's mine. I don't want you using up all its energy."

"Whatever."

He tried readjusting his backpack, but the straps cut into his shoulders. "It's gonna take forever to walk to Ashley's. My back could break."

"Toughen up, Canada boy."

He walked slowly across his kitchen, taking his last look, maybe making a last memory of his trailer. His home. As he reached for the doorknob, his hand shook. For a second, I didn't know whether I was afraid he'd change his mind or whether I was afraid he wouldn't. He pulled open the door and let it slam shut behind us. Slowly we walked down the gravel driveway, past the play dump, past Frank the Creeper's motorcycle, past the mailboxes and the faded sign that said, *River Estates Mobile Home Park*. He didn't look back, but I did. *Toughen up*, I told myself. *Toughen up, Canada girl.*

It was hot. Too hot for spring, and way too hot for morning. A pool of sweat formed between my shirt and backpack. Graham's hair was plastered flat from sweat and when he scratched his head, his hair stood up in short clumps.

We walked on the gravel shoulder and carefully moved into the grass when a car drove by. Finally we came to the intersection with the Rattlesnake Bar and Grill billboard. The sun had faded the picture, but you could still see two pretty girls with tank tops, arms wrapped around each other. Underneath the girls, the sign said, *Friends, food, and fun!* Not a word about beer or mozzarella sticks. Not far from the sign, the weeds turned into grass and the grass turned into a neighborhood.

"I'm so thirsty," I said.

"Try carrying a five-thousand-pound backpack."

"Toughen up, Canada boy."

"Stop saying that!"

"Who's going to carry the solar panels and fight grizzly bears?"

"Duh. The Chemist."

The clouds came together in big fluffs and

blocked the sun. Still, it felt hot, and the air was sticky.

"Our moms will be scared." I can't remember who said it, but it was probably me. I'm the one who would never want our moms to worry.

"Don't even start!" he said. "We'll call tonight when it's all done so they know we're safe. Just think about the Chemist. Don't let your head go anywhere else. The Chemist. Canada. Cinnamon bread with honey."

I stared at my feet. When my right foot came down on the sidewalk, I thought, *The*, and when the left one followed, I thought, *Chemist*. Like a drum, I marched. The! Chemist! The! Chemist! Right! Left! Right! Left!

* * *

We were two blocks from the brick house, which was divided into apartments. Every window had white blinds except one. A purple sheet or blanket covered the corner window on the first floor. That had to be Ashley's place.

I'd met Ashley, because Kari sometimes invited her over for pizza and movies. Kari felt sorry for Ashley, and maybe Ashley felt sorry for Kari. Graham hated their "girly-girl movies" because, he said, those movies made Kari and Ashley talk about boyfriends. And then they'd either get mad or sad. Graham liked adventure movies. I bet he thought running away would be an adventure movie starring him.

"Is this it?" I asked.

Graham pulled up his T-shirt to wipe his forehead sweat. "Yup. Purple window. That's it."

When we turned onto the sidewalk, a woman with deep frown lines slammed the front door and hustled by us, grumbling, "Damn that girl. Can't pay me enough." She stormed down the sidewalk. "Saint Bernard. Dumbest thing I ever heard."

* * *

From the hall, we heard bangs and shouts. The noise told me to wait, but Graham barged right into Ashley's apartment, so I followed him.

I got a quick look before we dropped to the floor: Ashley, by the couch, a stocking cap pulled completely over her eyes. Yelling. Stomping. Throwing things at the door, which is why we belly-crawled under the kitchen table, backpacks and all.

Something banged over our heads. I peeked. Ashley shouted, "It's my life!" A lamp flew across the room. "I don't care if this is a County apartment. I pay rent! I have a job! If I want a Saint Bernard, that's my business. Saint Bernards save lives!"

Graham cleared his throat, but he squeaked. "Ashley?"

"I want my money now! I'm not waiting until the first of the month. Screw you and your budget!"

Graham yelled this time. "Ashley!"

Ashley froze. Slowly, she lifted the stocking cap just above her eyelashes. She got on her knees and crawled under the table.

"Graham!" she shrieked. "And your friend what's-her-name!" She smooched Graham's forehead and mussed his hair. "Love the hair, dude!

You're so cool." She tried to hug him, backpack and all. Then she gave me a forehead kiss, too. "I don't remember your name, but I know your face. You're gorgeous and lovely. Like a preteen super-model."

I felt my face go red. "It's Daisy."

"A flower. So, so lovely. You deserve to be named after a flower." She put her elbows on the floor and rested her chin on her hands.

I said, "So do you!" And she smiled.

Graham cleared his throat again. "Ashley, we need your help."

"I bought fifty records at the thrift store. The Beatles . . . and the Clash and . . . a bunch of others. Stay here, and we'll listen to records all night. It'll be a hoot."

Graham tried to sit up, but he whacked his head on the table.

"You okay?" I asked.

"I bought a crap-ton of Beatles. I love how they sound on a real record player, even if they're scratched. I got some old grunge stuff, too."

Graham rubbed his head. "Here's the deal. We need a driver, and you're all we've got."

She straightened the knit cap on her head.

"We really, really need help," Graham said. "Really, really."

"Today I'm going to look for ... hmm ... what was that dog again? They're big."

"The Saint Bernard?" I asked.

"That's the one! They're so cute and cuddly. I don't care how much they cost to feed. We all gotta eat, right?"

"Ashley, please listen for just a second. We need a ride," Graham said. "Somebody's going to get hurt if we don't help."

"So you should call 911."

We'd hit nowhere at one hundred miles per hour. I had to take over.

"Ashley, you like Saint Bernards because they help people. You could be like a Saint Bernard and help save my dad's life."

She rolled on her back and sighed. "How's that going to happen?"

I said, "My dad is being blamed for something he didn't do. It was a total accident. So we're breaking him out of prison. It's not fair. He tried to put out the fire but it was too big and—"

Ashley squeezed my leg. "Your dad's in prison?"

"Yes. And he shouldn't be. It's wrong and unfair, and the fed-mates are going to hurt him. Bad. I'm breaking him out. No matter what. I need an escape driver. If you won't do it, then we'll have to drive ourselves. And we could end up hurt because we don't know how to drive."

"Prison?" She squinted.

I felt our chances gliding across the dirty linoleum and right out the door. Judge Henry, I had to be honest with her. You talked a lot about telling the truth, and that's exactly what I did.

"Yes. Prison, Ashley. He's in a real prison."

"Prison?" Ashley stared through me. I thought about waving my hand in front of her face, but I figured it was better to let her think about it. Then her eyes focused on me. "Everybody wants out of prison, but there's really no escape, is there?"

"It's a *low*-security prison. No chains or bars or cells. Just a big fence. We can do it. We've got a plan."

For a while, none of us spoke. I could hear the person next door running a vacuum. As we sat on the crusty floor, I thought Ashley should borrow that vacuum. A mop, too.

Ashley slithered backward and stood up. We did, too. She took a key from a hook on the wall. Over it was a handwritten note.

Rule Reminder #3: Do not drive unless there's a licensed driver in the car with you.

She thrust her left arm in the air. "Prison escape!"

Graham whispered, "Shhhh. We don't want anyone to hear that."

"I'll keep it on the down low," she whispered back. "So let's hit it."

"Ashley," I asked. "Do you want to pack some stuff?"

"Wait! I have to call in sick at work. It's my responsibility." She pulled a cell phone from her back pocket, one of those fancy phones that talks to you. "Call Thrift 'N' More." She winked at me. "Hey Bob! It's Ashley." Her voice was chirpy—too chirpy. "I can't make it in today. Strep throat."

Graham frowned and whispered, "Sound *sick*!"

Ashley's eyes got big. She cleared her throat and talked with a sandpaper voice, deep and scratchy. "And I sprained my ankle." Graham slapped the top of his head. Ashley looked at Graham like, *What?* Then she added, "And I puked."

She hung up. "Done and done! I'll pack and be out in a snap."

* * *

"This is a very long snap," I told Graham.

Graham tilted his head. "Maybe she said, 'I'll be back after my *nap*.'"

"We're going to miss Club Fed's smoke break if we don't fly. Go knock on her door," I said.

Then Ashley's bedroom door opened, and she came out dragging a black suitcase. It scraped against the old wood floor. She needed both hands and a grunt to move it. Ashley had changed into jeans, a red tank top, and a gray sweater. Her sunglasses were huge, and she'd covered her head with a black wig cut into a bob.

"It's not sunny anymore," Graham said. "You don't need your shades."

She dropped the suitcase with a thud and spun around like a ballerina. "This is my escape wardrobe."

DEAR JUDGE HENRY,

Ashley's car did not say, "I'm being driven by a hot babe with a bulging bank account." It said, "I'm a rusty Oldsmobile that clunk-clunk-clunks and spits black smoke from the tailpipe."

But the car had a bigger problem. The gas tank line was on red. Grandma and I stop for gas a lot, so I knew we were about to lose a chunk of the escape budget. Did we have enough money to buy gas to Canada? The sandwiches wouldn't last long. We'd need more food. How much did solar panels cost? Could we get enough food from hunting and fishing? I didn't even like fish *sticks*. How was I going to eat something from a lake with eyes and bones and scales? My head exploded with worries.

I asked, "Did you bring any money, Ashley?"

"I think I'm broke until the first of the month. But here. You can check." She tossed her purse to the back where Graham and I were sitting. We'd argued about who got to sit up front, but then I remembered a law about keeping kids in the backseat. We didn't want cops pulling us over for illegal seating. "Dig around and see what's in there."

Graham unzipped the small purse and made a sick face. Out came a comb stuck with a wad of gum. He emptied the bag between us: a paper advertising a Saint Bernard in need of a home (it said, "Cupcake is lovable but needs a firm hand"), two lollipops, a coupon for toilet paper, four lipsticks, a granola bar, eyeliner, and a refrigerator magnet that said, *"Help one person at a time, and always start with the person nearest you."*— *Mother Teresa.*

Graham looked at me and shrugged.

"Any green in there?" she asked.

"Nope." I sighed. "No money."

A few heavy raindrops plopped on the windshield. She leaned forward like she couldn't see and snapped at me, "Don't talk to me when it's raining!"

I kept quiet.

Finally we stopped at the little gas station on the edge of town, the one where Grandma buys cigarettes. Ashley filled the tank, and Graham and I went inside with my birthday money. A lady with gray hair and thick glasses stood behind the cash register. She wore a sweatshirt stitched with the words *St. Bridget Church*, and a long cross necklace dangled halfway to her waist.

"Pump one," I told her and put the cash on the counter. I kept my hand on it, though.

She stared at Graham. "My goodness, young man, what happened to your hair?"

"Um . . . it's growing out because . . . it fell out." He ran his fingers from his neck to the top of his head, and he looked like a peacock with very short feathers. "It fell out because . . . because . . ."

The lady did a little gasp. "Chemo?"

We nodded at the same time. She said, "Oh, you poor boy. Where—I mean, what kind of cancer is it, honey?"

Graham blinked a bunch of times and blurted out, "Ear."

"Ear cancer?" she repeated.

"Yes," I said as serious as possible.

"Why, I've never heard of such a thing!"

I put my hand on Graham's shoulder. "It's very, very rare and very, very bad."

"Oh, dear." Her face turned a little red. "I'm sorry. I didn't mean to—" Graham put his hand by his ear and interrupted. "WHAT? I CAN'T HEAR YOU!"

"Tell you what," she said, clutching her cross necklace. "You kids can take a donut from the case in the back. I recommend the ones with chocolate frosting. And it's on me."

I grabbed Graham's arm to stop the donut leap and tapped the counter with my other hand. "Ma'am, lots of people offer to help. They say all kinds of nice things, but, I'm embarrassed to say this, nothing ever comes of it. They probably just forget about their kind offers. Thank you so much for your gift of donuts, but we actually can't have *donuts*. Carbs are bad for ear cancer. If you want to help, really help, then you could think about doing what Jesus would do and pay for our gas. Because our mom spends all of her money on co-pays and medicine." Her eyes grew big, and her mouth kind of hung open. I continued, "We could cover an entire co-pay for the cost of that gas." She tilted her head and I asked, "You're a grownup. You know what a co-pay is, don't you?"

"Yes, dear." Her voice was tight. "Do you?"

"I sure do," I said. "It's when the County stops paying your doctor bills because your mom gets a job, then your mom has bad insurance and every time you get a sniffle she has to write a check for the co-pay at the doctor, and it's usually just a virus anyway, not the real flu, and all that money is gone and you don't even have a prescription."

Graham looked at me and said, "WHAT?"

"I told her we don't have a lot of money." As I spoke, I moved my hands like sign language.

Graham nodded. "EVEN THE COUNTY WON'T HELP," he said.

The lady's lips were small and puckered. She looked at the poor boy with cancer. She looked at me, sad, sweet, cute little me. I clutched my money.

Finally, she cleared her throat and said, "Perhaps I can help this one time."

I tucked the birthday money in my pocket. On the way out the door, Graham and I each took a donut, plus one for Ashley.

DEAR JUDGE HENRY,

Graham told a whale-sized lie. Ear cancer! Sometimes he's so stupid. At least that lady had a job, and she could afford gas. That's probably what Graham was thinking when he started the lie. It wasn't my fault. I took over only because I knew his brain would freeze.

After we got gas, it rained harder. Because we were on the back roads, Graham sat up front with the map, and I sat in back. Ashley squeezed the steering wheel, leaned forward, and muttered to herself. Graham led us down country roads to avoid cop cars. The prison was only forty-five minutes away, and we'd spent at least that amount of time driving but getting nowhere. All Graham's directions were wrong. We passed the same barn three times.

Graham wouldn't admit he didn't know how to read the map. "It's not the same barn. The other one had a fence around it."

"There was no fence," I told him. "It's the same barn."

Ashley pounded the steering wheel. "Your map is wrong!"

"The map's fine." I leaned forward and got in Graham's face. "*He* can't follow a black line."

Graham threw the map at me. "If you're so smart, you figure it out."

"I'm definitely the brains of this operation."

"More like the butt of this operation," he said.

I wanted to smack his head. He's the one who said to use back roads, since the car burped smoke and Ashley didn't have the gift of driving the speed limit. The County is messed up. They gave *Ashley* a driver's license.

And now we were closer to lost than to Club Fed. I yelled at Graham, "You're the King of Stupid!"

"You're the Queen of Stupid."

"Sooooo original! Can't imagine how you came up with that one," I said.

"Daisy Bauer. Queen of Not Knowing the Difference in Barns."

"Graham Cracker. King of Not Reading a Map."

Then, like a mom yelling at us to "Stop it right now or else," the sky exploded. *Boom. Bam.* Thunder and rain—rain so hard it sounded like a thousand hammers on the car's roof. The windshield looked like the shower door in my grandma's bathroom, blurry and white, with some shadows that could be the road and could be some trees.

Ashley put her hands over her face and screamed.

"Hey!" Graham reached over and took hold of the steering wheel. "Stop the car, Ashley."

"I can't see."

"It's generally recommended to keep your eyes open and your hands on the wheel."

I didn't like Graham's calm. "Turn on the wipers!"

Graham clicked something by the steering wheel. The wipers ran fast, but they couldn't keep up with the gush of water on the windshield.

"I can't see," she said. "We're gonna get hit. We're gonna GET HIT!" Her breathing came hard and fast.

I felt the car come to a stop. "You can't stop in the middle of the road."

"It's a gravel road," Graham said. "Nobody's out here."

The car swayed in a blast of wind, and suddenly it was dark. Ashley wouldn't take her hands off her face. Her shoulders shook. "Driving in the rain is dangerous. It's bad. It's bad."

Graham turned on the overhead light as a branch slapped the back window. "What should we do?"

"Turn on the radio. Push the button until you hear a weather voice," I said.

Graham pushed the radio button. Country. Another push. Dance mix. Another push. More country. More dance mix. A jewelry store commercial. Finally, a weather voice. ". . . seek shelter immediately. Severe thunderstorms can produce straight-line winds and tornadoes with little warning. This path of super cells is traveling west-southwest at thirty miles an hour. If you do not have a basement, seek shelter in an interior room without windows . . ."

"Tornadoes?" Ashley grabbed the wheel, stomped the gas, and the car roared forward. "We gotta hide."

"Turn the radio off," I told Graham. "It's making her freak out."

Ashley braked hard, and the car skidded and stopped. She took off her sweater and wrapped it around her head, over her eyes.

Graham whirled around. "Ashley's brain cells are flying outta her ears!" Damn if he wasn't right.

The wind turned to a howl. High-pitched and wobbly, like the pretend ghost noises you make during a scary story. *Whoooo . . . whoooo . . .* The wind was making fun of us. *Stupid, stupid kids.*

"Now what?" I whispered.

I don't think Graham could hear me, but he

wiggled around and pulled something from his pocket. He licked it and pressed his hand against his forehead. "The Idea Coin!" he shouted. He froze for a few seconds. Then he turned to Ashley. "Keep moving forward. Take it slow. I'll look out the side window." She didn't take the sweater off her head and eyes, but she followed his commands. "Slower! No, faster than that! Good, good. A little more to the right."

The car bucked and bolted, slowed and sputtered. Rain and wind beat the car.

"I think it's a house. Turn here!"

A turn, followed by more howling, a thump, and a bump. The car stopped. Ashley turned the engine off. Everything was silent for a moment—a second of nothing, no engine, no wind, nothing but breathing. Graham slipped the coin in his pocket. Then a blast of lightning and thunder rocked the car.

Ashley screamed. Graham screamed. I screamed. Suddenly the doors were open. Ashley had both hands on Graham's back because she couldn't see. He ran. She clutched his shirt and followed. I ran, too. The car was in a yard, about ten feet from a white house with a front porch. Graham banged on the door and tried to open it, but it was locked.

"Is it a house?" Ashley shouted through her sweater.

He banged some more. "Yeah, it's a house."

I pushed the doorbell over and over. Nothing.

Then another crash of lightning hit so close, the hair on my arm tingled. Ashley screamed, "Break the window! Kick in the door!"

Graham pointed at a truck in the driveway. "Hold my arm, Ashley! Follow me."

I had no idea why we'd get in a pickup truck, having just escaped a car, but Ashley did the clutch-and-run, and I raced behind them. He opened the truck's door, looked inside, and pressed a garage door opener. Sure enough, the garage door opened. We ran into the garage. Graham hit another button on the wall, and the garage door closed and shut out the storm.

We huddled together by a door leading to the house. The garage was stuffed with a rusty little car and a heap of junk: bikes, a picnic table, lawn chairs, a lawn mower, a tool chest, cardboard boxes, big recycling bins.

Graham raised his eyebrow. "So who's *not* the King of Stupid?"

I didn't answer. I wandered through the garage, shivering and checking for things that might help. There was a bow and arrow hanging from the wall. But none of us knew how to use it. A shovel. A shovel could help. I leaned it against the door. Hammer? Sure.

"Good idea." Graham started poking through boxes.

A bowling ball? Maybe. Christmas lights? Not so much.

"I'm cold! I'm hungry!" Ashley's face was still covered with the sweater. The garage door rattled in the wind. We flinched when lightning walloped nearby.

"We need a safe basement," Ashley said. "I'm cold. I'm hungry. I need a blanket."

Graham turned the handle on the door leading to the house. The door opened, and the house invited us in. More or less.

DEAR JUDGE HENRY,

We called, "Hello? Can you help us?" No voice answered, but I swear there was a *feeling*. The house seemed to smile and open its arms and say, "Come. Be warm and dry and safe. Go to my basement." If those people had been home, they would *not* have told two cute kids and a nice lady with a wet sweater on her head to stand in the lightning. You said yourself they are perfectly nice people who just happened to have the wrong house in the wrong place at the wrong time. Perfectly nice people would have said, "Come. Be warm and dry and safe. Go to our basement." Besides, we dripped puddles on the pretty wood floor, and that was rude.

We found the basement right away—it was off the kitchen. I led Ashley down the stairs. The basement was old and dark and damp, but it had a laundry room and a faded couch against the wall.

"You can take that off now. We're safe," I told Ashley. She unraveled it slowly. Rain had soaked right through the sweater. The black-bob wig twisted and clung to her head like a second skin.

"Graham, please get my suitcase from the trunk," she said.

"Are you kidding?"

"No. I need different hair. Go get it."

Even I didn't want Graham fried up by lightning. "Ashley, we'll get it after the storm, okay?"

She said, "It's not okay. I need hair. This wig is ruined. I need my hair. Graham, don't you understand? My suitcase has my hair."

"Fine," he said. "Give me the keys."

"I think they're still in the car."

He slouched up the steps. "Graham!" I said. "This is stupid. Get back here! I mean it!"

Graham acted like he didn't hear me. I wanted to rip Ashley's wig off her head and smack her with it. We shivered and waited. As long as he was risking his life, I hoped he'd remember to bring the backpacks. We had clothes for the Chemist, and I wanted to change, too. We could all buy new clothes once we crossed into Canada.

I'd never seen Ashley close up, except for when we hid under her table. I wasn't paying attention to her face then. I had the bigger job of convincing her to be our escape driver.

A long scar ran from ear to chin, like someone had drawn it with a red marker. I knew there were scars under the wig hair, too. Still, she was pretty, even with scars and fake hair.

I heard a thud and saw Graham's feet. He dragged the suitcase one thump at a time. He was re-soaked. Rainwater dripped down his face. With the suitcase leaning against his leg, he lifted his shirt and wiped his face, which only spread water around. The suitcase was black but covered with stickers. Peace sign stickers. Smiley face stickers. Sleeping Beauty stickers. Stickers that said, "Rock On" and "Well-behaved women rarely make history."

Graham grunted. "Wigs do not weigh one hundred pounds. What's in here?"

Ashley sighed. "Just hurry, please."

He dragged the suitcase to her feet. She unzipped it and tossed back the flap. I couldn't believe it. There were wigs and hats and scarves and some clothes, but not many. Mostly the suitcase was packed with *records*. On top of the pile: The Beatles' *Sgt. Pepper*. The Chemist's favorite.

She twirled again, but it was a clumsy and drippy twirl. "This *was* my escape wardrobe. Now I need to improvise."

"We're cold, too. Can we wear something of yours?"

She shook her head. "I'm tall and thin. I'm grown up. My things wouldn't fit either of you."

* * *

So, Judge Henry, what would *you* do if you were drenched and freezing and next to a laundry room? You'd poke through the dry old-people clothes and find something to wear. To borrow. You have to believe me: I would never, ever steal clothes from a grandmother, not even a fashionista grandma like mine.

We *borrowed*. I found a floppy pink nightgown with little baby roses. It smelled like grandma powder. My feet warmed quickly in thick gray socks that went to my knees. Graham put on a John Deere T-shirt and jeans that still had a belt in the loops. Good thing, too, because even when he tightened the belt, those pants dangled on his hips. He rolled up the pant legs so they didn't drag on the floor. We put our clothes in the dryer with little white sheets from a box called "Powder Fresh."

Ashley made us wait on the dusty couch while she sorted through their clothes. I don't know why since she had her own. Graham and I stared at the wall and listened to the storm. Even Graham sat frozen, and that is a miracle.

"I feel like Goldilocks and the Three Bears," I said.

Ashley called out, "A fashion statement unlike any other!" and stepped from the laundry room. She had a new wig—long and blond with pink highlights. And bangs. Always bangs. She thrust out her hip, showing off a man's T-shirt tucked into a blue skirt with white flowers. She'd twisted and tied the elastic waist into a knot so it wouldn't drop from her skinny hips. "All the way from Paris. Made from the finest silk. Designed by the world's best designer. You like?"

I asked, "If you have other clothes, why are you wearing their stinky stuff?"

"I feel bad being the only comfortable person. It seems more fair, don't you think?"

"Now what?" Graham asked.

Ashley said, "There's a phone in the kitchen."

"No!" I bolted from sitting to standing. "No phones! We're not calling anybody. I know this isn't going according to plan, but we'll fix it. We're going to wait for dry clothes and wait for the storm to be over. Then we'll leave. Don't even try to talk to me about it."

"I thought we could order pizza," Ashley said.

My stomach growled. Nobody delivered pizza to people on gravel roads. The peanut butter sandwiches were in the car, but the storm scared us, and we should save our food if we could. "Maybe . . . maybe . . ."

"Maybe what?" Graham's voice demanded action.

"Maybe we should go upstairs and make something to eat."

Graham shook his head. "They might come home."

"If they come home, they'll either find us in the basement or the kitchen. What's the difference? We'll tell them the truth. We got lost in a storm. We're hungry, and you have ear cancer."

Nobody argued.

*　*　*

We ate canned pineapple, baked beans, and pickles, and then we shared a box of cinnamon-flavored cereal without milk.

"Tastes like cinnamon toast." Graham was happy again. He pointed at the picture on the wall by the table. It was Jesus and the Last Supper.

"Check it out! They probably would have given us all this food because they're church people."

Ashley tossed her blond-and-pink locks over her shoulder and blew a kiss at the picture. "Thank you Jesus and friends!"

The thunder rumbled from a distance now, and the rain only pitter-pattered.

Graham looked at me. "We could probably go."

"No!" Ashley slapped her hands on the table. "No driving in the rain. No driving! In the rain!"

"We can't stay here," he said. "So what now, Daisy?"

"I don't know. This isn't in the notebook."

"Well, you better figure it out!"

"Why don't you figure it out?" I yelled.

"Because the Chemist is *your* dad!"

"Who's the Chemist?" Ashley asked.

The worries were back in my head, but bigger than before. What a nightmare. Getting lost. The storm. The time. We'd missed the smoke break at Club Fed. We'd already stayed too long at the farmhouse. When were the church people coming home? Where would we sleep?

Kari had probably noticed we were gone by now—really gone, not just goofing around. And she probably was looking for us already, probably wondering if Frank the Creeper had us locked away. And that was good. If we'd left a note, she'd have clues instead of suspecting Frank the Creeper. The longer the cops talked to Kari—and maybe to Frank the Creeper—the more time we had.

Graham slapped his hand on the table. When he lifted his palm, the Idea Coin gleamed under the kitchen light.

"The Idea Coin. Use it."

"I don't know. What if I burn up the energy? We might need it later." Still, I put my finger on it. My whole hand tingled.

Ashley looked at me, then Graham. "What's an Idea Coin?"

"I don't think we have a choice," Graham said. "I did it last time. You go."

"Who's the Chemist and what's an Idea Coin?"

"Daisy's dad is the Chemist," Graham told Ashley, "and the coin is our way outta this crap-crusted mess."

"Don't chemists pollute the world with chemicals?" Ashley said. "You sure he doesn't belong in prison?"

"The Chemist is the other kind of chemist. He makes experiments."

"So he's cool?"

"He's the best chemist in the world." I meant Dad, but he was the Chemist forever and ever.

"Then he shouldn't be locked up," Ashley said. "Why do people have to be in prison for things that aren't their fault?"

"Right on, Sister Ashley!" Graham high-fived her.

I was done talking about the Chemist. The Idea Coin. It called to me.

The coin shimmered pretty well for being created in 1919. I used my finger to drag it to the edge of the table. I clutched it in my right hand and pressed it against my heart. Then I licked it and stuck it to my forehead and closed my eyes. When I opened them, the first thing I saw was the refrigerator. It was white and covered with magnets and pictures and pieces of paper. And a calendar.

The refrigerator tugged at me, I swear. It seemed to call me, to ask for me, to promise me a secret. I stood and shuffled across the kitchen. My eyes went right to the calendar. A long line was drawn in red ink between Wednesday's *8:30 Marv, Dr. Owen* and the next Monday's *Noon, meet Nancy, Golden Spoon Buffet.* Above it was one word: *Orlando!* Yes, with an exclamation point.

"They're not here!" I shouted. "They're in Orlando until Sunday."

I whirled around and looked at the section of wall between the refrigerator and the door. There was a rack with keys and a long blue sign above it with white letters: "God bless this happy house." Below the key rack was a long white sign with blue letters: "Saints are sinners who kept on going."

"They *are* church people! 'Saints are sinners who kept on going.' Happy church people who want to be saints!"

Then, on the counter, right in front of the toaster, I saw two twenty-dollar bills and a piece of scrap paper that read *Thanks!* in the same red ink. "You're welcome," I whispered and picked up the money. I didn't have any pockets, so I took the cash to Graham who was still at the table, stuffing dry cereal into his mouth. He smiled and tucked the money in his pocket.

"Where's Ashley?" I asked.

He shrugged. "Bathroom?"

Didn't matter. I felt light and loose. Back in the kitchen, my brain popped with ideas. We could stay overnight and get the Chemist tomorrow. If we needed to, we could hide out here with the Chemist. At least until Sunday. We could take a bunch of food and clothes and sheets and towels for the cabin. Maybe we'd find more money. I poked around the kitchen drawers. They were church people. They'd understand. We would borrow from them. The Chemist could send them a check and a thank-you note after we got to Canada.

The coin was still stuck to my forehead. I pressed it hard to help the ideas keep coming, and it worked. My brain was working at full speed. Maybe we could get jobs on the Internet and buy groceries instead of fishing. Maybe Graham's ear-cancer story would get us free gas all the way to Canada. Maybe Grandma would send us money.

I heard a clink and saw a metallic blur rush toward the refrigerator. I patted my head and, sure enough, it was gone. The Idea Coin had fallen off my forehead and disappeared under the refrigerator.

"Graham, it fell off my head! Help!"

DEAR JUDGE HENRY,

Refrigerators are heavy. Real heavy. We did not want to move that beast, but we had no choice. We needed that coin to save the Chemist. We grunted and groaned but only managed to pull it about one foot from the wall. Then I crawled over the countertop and squished behind it. Graham pulled from the front. I pushed from the back. We had to unplug it to move it a couple of feet, right in the middle of the kitchen. Underneath where it once stood were hairballs and dust and dead bugs and crumbs and a dried bread crust. But no Idea Coin.

Graham said we had to lift the refrigerator. *Graham* said we had to inspect the bottom because it's probably built with a magnet, and the coin had stuck to it. *Graham* went into the garage and got a car jack. *Graham* put the jack under the refrigerator's bottom and pumped it until the refrigerator started to lift, and then tip. These ideas came from Graham's mini-brain.

At first, the refrigerator tipped forward, toward Graham, with its bottom resting on the jack. Balanced. Almost perfectly balanced. I was afraid to slide my hand under it, though—afraid it might slip off the jack and flatten my hand.

I told him, "Maybe you should come back here and feel around for it."

"No way. I'm not putting my hand down there. I'm not crunching my bones."

"Nice. So I should crunch mine?"

"I need my hands to hunt and fish." He poked me. "You dropped it, Queen of Dropping Coins. So you look for it."

I called from behind the beast, "Fine. But try to hold it steady. Don't let it drop back on me. I'm serious. Do *not* let it fall."

"I won't. I'll balance the weight more toward me. I know my arms look skinny," he grunted, "but they're strong. Don't worry."

That's when I should have worried. Because as soon as Graham pulled on the refrigerator, the whole thing started tilting away from me and toward him. It was slow motion, I swear. The refrigerator fell to the floor like a leaf drops to the ground. The air seemed to prop it up for a few seconds, and if there had been a wind, it might have swirled. Then there was a massive non-leaf-like crash.

"Damn!" Graham shouted.

"Are you under there?" I covered my eyes because I was afraid he'd been pancaked.

"Duh. I'm right here."

Now I could be mad. "I said to balance it, not let it drop!"

His eyes were huge. "I pulled just a little, so it wouldn't fall on your hand. That's all."

"Well, now what, King of Dropping Refrigerators?"

"What happened?" Ashley, who'd disappeared during the coin search, came in from the dining room. She wasn't alone. Mud formed a trail behind her and a *dog*.

And, man, he stunk! The smell was like the part of the zoo where elephant poop steams in the sun, like a dare to put your face in the litter box, like when Alex leaves the bathroom after eating chili.

"Where've you been?" Graham asked.

"Woof." This dog was huge and scruffy, mostly brown with some black splotches. His ears were pointy and lopsided. Not the kind of dog from a cute birthday card. Ashley got on her knees. He put his paws on her shoulders and licked her face. "This is exactly the kind of dog I was looking for. Isn't he a sweet-licious baby?"

"I thought you wanted a Saint Bernard." I plugged my nose. "Where did you find that disgusting thing?"

"Are you out of your mind? Saint Bernards are huge! Do you know how much they eat?" She scratched the dog's ears. "I saw this sweetheart from the window. I went outside, and he gave me a tour. He'd been hiding. He showed me a barn and some big trees and the pretty hedge. He showed me how many branches came down during the storm. And he showed me his Beefy Bits and—oh boy, you'd do anything for those, wouldn't ya?"

Ashley kissed the tip of his nose and pulled a nugget from a Beefy Bit bag. The dog's tail went wild. He jumped at Ashley and snarfed the treat right out of her hand. "Good boy! Were ya scared, muffin? Huh? Were ya? You're safe now."

Graham plugged his nose. I said, "Stinkbomb!"

Ashley's mouth opened. I figured she couldn't stand breathing through her nose. Turns out, she was mad. "That's sooooo mean! Dog hater!"

"It's not mean. It's true!" I said. "Why do we have to call things something they're not? Because it's nice? I'm sick of nice. I'd rather have *true*. Play dump, not playground, right Graham?"

He didn't answer.

"Nobody calls their dog Stinkbomb, Daisy," Ashley said. "He has a tag, but there's no name or number. Anything that was printed on it wore off."

"We have a bigger problem." I pointed at the refrigerator. "Look what Graham did!"

"I didn't do it! You're the one who pushed!"

Ashley stood and crossed her arms. "It's all

about you, you, you! I'm keeping this dog and giving him a name."

"Can you name him *after* we get the refrigerator fixed?" I asked.

"No. I can't." Ashley got back on her knees and hugged the beast. "I'm not helping someone who's mean to my dog and mean to my cousin. You have to defend your friends, Daisy. Don't you know that? I'm taking Fred upstairs until you're ready to say you're sorry." She shook the Beefy Bits bag and "Fred" pranced after her, barking like a maniac for his treat.

I crossed my arms. "She's the worst partner ever!"

Graham turned to me and said, "Her head is messed up, and it won't ever heal right. You *are* mean, Daisy Bauer."

I leaned forward and yelled at him, "Am not! *You* are mean. You pull my hair!"

"You'd suck the nice out of a puppy!"

Now that was a good line, and my mouth wanted to fire back, but I couldn't think of anything equal, except "You'd suck the nice out of a kitten," and that would be the stupidest thing to say. Ever.

Then my brain came up with words, and they shot out my mouth. "If I'm so mean how come I have friends and you don't have any!"

Right away I wanted to take it back. I wished I had a net to catch those words before they got to his ears.

Graham's eyes flashed sad and mad but mostly mad. His hands curled into fists, and I thought he wanted to hit me. I dashed to the dining room, to the other side of the table. He followed and in seconds we were circling the table. Tigers ready to pounce.

I tried some different words, words to help forget the other words. "If I'm so mean, what are you doing here? Why are you going to Club Fed?"

"I'm a friend helping a friend helping her dad." He said *friend* like he meant *turd*. "You don't know what friend means. You're clueless."

"I'm not clueless!"

"Free of clues. That's what you are."

"Stop it right now, Graham Cracker!"

"Or what? You'll watch Jesse push me? You'll ignore me at lunch? You'll pretend you don't hear Alice call me 'spaz boy'?"

Judge Henry, I wish I could tell you Graham was a whiner and a fake. But I'd done all those things. When you asked me if I had any shame, I tell you, cross my heart and hope to die, my shame then and there almost burst my body into flames.

Graham stared at me. I bit my lip and looked at the floor. The quiet made me burn even hotter.

I said, "We have to find that coin."

Graham's voice was growly. "Move."

So I moved. He sat on the kitchen floor and inspected the bottom of the refrigerator, poking and pulling at cords and coils. His fingers came out covered with grease and spiderwebs.

I knelt beside him. "Nothing?"

"You sure it went *under* the refrigerator?"

"I'm sure! Two hundred percent!" I poked and pulled in all the places he'd just poked and pulled.

Graham kicked the refrigerator. "Now what?"

Tears trickled down the front of my granny gown. I ran past the tipped-on-the-door refrigerator, through the dining room, and out the front door. I ran. I ran across the driveway, across the grass, and into the old barn. The door opened with a creak and slammed behind me.

DEAR JUDGE HENRY,

Alone in the barn I couldn't hear anything but my sniffles and the *blop blop blop* of rain hitting the roof. I hate crying in front of people, except for my mom, who's good at back rubs. I wiped my eyes and nose on the floppy pink granny gown. My feet were wet and cold.

The barn was full of stink and junk—yard junk and farm junk and Fred stink. In the corner, right next to the door, were some smelly old pillows, huge bowls of water, and dog food. Fred's little home. I curled up on the pillow.

I'd ruined everything. The Idea Coin was lost, and we weren't going far without it. If fed-mates can't figure out how to escape from Club Fed, how could I? They were smart enough to hack computers and steal tax money. I was just a stupid kid. Queen Stupid.

The Idea Coin had *something*. I felt it. Graham

felt it. Addison Kramer, who used to live by us, showed me her rock collection this one time. She said rocks and minerals hold energy and memories and history. Maybe the Idea Coin was like that. It's been on Earth since 1919. That's a lot of energy.

When did the *Titanic* sink? Maybe the Idea Coin was on the *Titanic* and it sunk in the ocean and was eaten by a fish and the fish was caught by a fishing fleet and when the fish cutter split the fish, he found the coin and kept it. The Idea Coin might have traveled all over the world. Maybe it went from Spain to Utah to China. Maybe Grandma found it on the sidewalk and used it for cigarettes. Maybe it was in Mom's change jar, *in my very own trailer*, and she spent it, and it traveled to Graham's uncle, who brought it back. So many possibilities. So many memories. So much energy.

Without the Idea Coin, we were screwed. And the Chemist? I shivered and thought about terrible things happening to the Chemist.

* * *

It felt like an hour had passed when Graham opened the door. He turned on a dim light.

"Hey," he said.

"Hey yourself."

Graham frowned when he saw the Fred corner. "These church people don't love their dog! Leaving him alone for five days with slime water—look, there are bugs floating in it."

Graham picked bugs out of Fred's dish and flicked them across the floor. I was afraid he'd come to say he and Ashley were going home. Then what? No Idea Coin, no Graham, no Ashley, no car.

No escape for the Chemist.

Something snorted. Graham scrambled up and peeked over the stalls. "Oh, my God, Daisy! Check it out!"

"What?"

"Horses!" His voice squeaked from excitement.

I jumped up and peeked with Graham. A

brown pony looked up at us and swished its tail. In the next stall was a white pony, and the one next to it had black spots. "Ponies!" I said. "Soooo cute!"

Graham inspected them. "Not ponies. Miniature horses. They might be exactly what we need, and they're small. Way easier to handle than big horses."

"Cuter than puppies!"

I patted the pony's nose, and Graham rubbed its ear. "Who leaves animals for five days? That's abuse," he said. "If I were those people, I'd rent a trailer and bring my animals and stay on a farm instead of a hotel."

"A Jesus picture doesn't make you a real church person. Just another fake."

He didn't call me a fake friend, and he didn't seem so mad. We scratched and stroked the ponies. They nibbled on our hands, looking for a treat. The wind howled through the trees. Thankfully we had a house for sleeping. But then what? When night turned into morning and morning turned into the Club Fed smoke break, and it was me—just me—then what?

Graham said, "I got two things to tell you. The first is we both got Mom messages on my cell."

"I don't want to hear it." I shivered.

"You have to listen before I tell you the second thing."

"Why?"

"Because."

"Just tell me."

He got his phone from his back pocket. "There are two from your mom. Listen."

"No!" I sat on Fred's pillow and plugged my ears.

"You gotta listen. That's the only way I'll know if you're gonna stick around. Because we got decisions to make."

Graham was wondering whether *I* was going to stick around? I felt lighter, but only for a second, because he pushed that cell phone against my ear. It was Mom's you're-in-deep-trouble voice. "Daisy, call Kari. Now. Leaving without a note or phone call? That is NOT cool. I know you're mad about my vacation, but get over it or I will ground you for the entire summer!"

I pushed the phone away. "Enough. So what?"

"That's an old one. Here's the new one."

I yelled, "What difference does it make?"

"I need you to hear it so I know!" Graham shouted. "I need to know if you're a big fat chicken who's going to cry about Mommy! Because I'm not. I don't wanna go back to school. I'm not going back to the play dump or any of it. There's nothing for us back there. Nothing. I can't even think of all the things I don't want to go back to."

I took the phone and closed my eyes as Mom's voice began, soft and shaky. "Honey . . . I'm praying you ran off and that . . . that you're safe somewhere. I'm sorry if I hurt you. Please call me or Kari." She paused. "When I quit drinking, I quit because of you. I knew if I didn't quit, I wouldn't get to be your mom anymore. And that's the most important thing. Being your mom. God, please be safe, baby. Here's Alex. He wants to say something."

He said, "Hey, buddy. You're scaring us. Just call. Nobody's going to be mad. Nobody's going to punish you. We'll just come get you, no questions asked. Your mom . . . your mom's feeling real bad. Me, too, and—"

I tossed the phone to Graham. "I don't want to hear any more."

"See? See why you had to hear it? Because you're going to miss her! And her smoochy boyfriend, too."

"Like you're not going to miss your mom?"

"I got an idea. We can talk to them every day on the Internet. If they see our faces and know we're safe, they won't care where we are. They can have their lives, and we'll have ours. They want boyfriends and friends. Better jobs and not so many bills. Mom won't shut up about how much I cost."

"Everything's messed up." I sat back on the Fred pillow and pulled my legs into the nightgown.

"Everything's always messed up. We roll with it. So what?" he said.

"People with cars that start can roll with it. In our case, *it* rolls over *us*."

He sat next to me on the stinky pillow. "You're wrong! Remember when we wanted to surprise our moms with some cool food and we lit those candles and one fell over and set the napkin on fire?"

I didn't get the point. "The place would've burned up if I didn't grab the pot and dump it on the table. And your mom slipped on all those wet macaroni noodles! And the fire made a black stain on the tablecloth my mom just bought at Thrift 'N' More."

"Right."

"Right? What's your point?"

"We fixed the problem. Daisy, everything about us is messy. Clothes. Hair."

"Speak for yourself! My grandma's a stylist."

"Rusty trailers. Frank the Creeper and his beer bottles."

I thought about the clankity clank of those beer bottles in the wind. And Mrs. Mundez, and the smell of lard and refried beans. And the cold winter that wrapped icy arms around our trailer.

Graham said, "You know what I mean?"

I nodded. "Car batteries dying halfway to the grocery store. Mom using nickels from the coin jar to buy milk because she's out of dimes. *Nickels!* I want to crawl under the counter and *die*."

"See? It ain't easy. Ever. The worst thing of all? Thrift-store shoes."

"Yes!" I yelled. "Thrift-store shoes! They smell like . . . like . . ."

"They smell how feet would smell if feet had butts!"

We laughed so hard my stomach hurt.

After the laughs were out, I felt my chin shaking. "Why is it always messy and hard for us? Why can't the easy stuff be big and stay a long time?"

Graham shrugged and kicked at the dead bugs he'd flicked out of Fred's water.

"On the voicemail, Alex said if we came back,

we wouldn't get punished and they wouldn't ask any questions."

"Do you believe him?" he said.

I thought for a minute. "Yes. I believe Alex."

"So you're going back?"

"I kinda want to, but I can't. The Chemist. We need each other. But maybe you should go back. Maybe Ashley should."

"You can't do it without us," Graham said.

I knew it was true.

"And there was a second thing I need to tell you." He reached into his pocket. "I found it."

The Idea Coin. He held it between his thumb and finger and showed me. I tried to grab it, but Graham backed away and put it in his pocket. "I found it under the rug by the sink. It must have rolled under the refrigerator and bounced out. It was there the whole time, sticking out from the rug."

"Let me see it."

"Umm . . . hmm . . . let's review. Did I lose the Idea Coin? Or was it you?"

"I accept complete and total responsibility." I jumped up and down and screamed and hugged Graham. "You! Are! Amazing! Graham, you're a rock star plus a world-champion wrestler multiplied by three superheroes and Harry Potter times ten."

He turned red and looked at the ceiling.

It was creepifying that I'd hugged him like that. I needed words to escape the weirdness and quick.

"I . . . like . . . ponies."

"Me, too!" Graham finally looked at me. "Ponies. Horses. Even donkeys."

"Me, too." I picked straw off the pink granny gown. "So this means we're back, right?"

"We're back."

"Today was just for practice. Tomorrow, it's the Graham Cracker Plot."

I snapped off the light and the barn went dark. Graham pulled hard on the barn door and as it closed behind us, I heard him mumble, "Only you get to call me that, you know."

DEAR JUDGE HENRY,

After the phone messages and horse discovery, the rain stopped. The storm had turned the yard into mud soup. Our feet squished in the grass. But we could see fine through the darkness. Ashley had turned on every light in the house. I could hear something, too. A low, steady thumping.

Through the living room window we saw Ashley slow dancing with her arms wrapped around herself. Once we got close, I recognized the song. "Oh, Darling." The Beatles.

Ashley spun in a circle. Her skirt and hair whirled. She was beautiful, a spinning doll with silk ribbons for hair. She lifted her arms and moved like a ballerina. Then she did something that made me feel sad. She wrapped her arms around the floor lamp. She swayed and danced with it and rested her head on the shade. She'd found a dance partner.

Then I had an idea so perfect my head about

popped off my body. The Chemist should marry Ashley! He described himself as "totally chill," so he could handle her when the crazies hit. He'd just wait it out, wait until everything was fine again. He'd like her music and her pink highlights. And her eyes. Ashley's eyes held a secret. *Guess who I was before this. Guess.*

DEAR JUDGE HENRY,

As soon as Graham and I stepped inside the house, Ashley grabbed our hands.

"The church people have an actual record player! We escaped to heaven!" She jumped up and down and clapped. "Do you like to dance?"

Graham said no at the exact time I said yes.

I twirled in a circle, just like she'd done. Except I kept my hands pressed on my sides so the granny gown didn't flip and show my undies. "Once, the Chemist took me to the Rattlesnake and it was almost the time when kids have to leave. When is that, Graham?"

"Nine o'clock."

"Right. Almost nine. The Chemist played country songs on the jukebox and taught me the Electric Slide. People watched and clapped and the bartender didn't kick me out until nine-thirty."

"The Chemist likes music?" Ashley asked.

"The Chemist loves music! He loves music so

much he even likes Mozart, and nobody likes Mozart, except music teachers."

She squeezed my hand. "Does the Chemist like to dance?"

"He dances. He sings. He plays drums. He *loves* music."

"Does he love cats? Because I want a cat. I want to own a pet store."

I shrugged. I thought, *Thank God the church people don't have any cats!* And, *I hope she doesn't see the ponies.*

Ashley turned around and fumbled with the records. She started a new song and cranked the sound. "Twist and Shout."

Ashley grabbed one of Graham's arms, and I grabbed the other, and we twisted and shouted all over that house. Ashley rolled up *Ladies Home Journal* and sang into it like a microphone. We twisted our way upstairs into the bedroom. The church people had the best jumping bed ever—huge, fluffy, white. We jumped so high we could touch the ceiling.

When the song ended, Ashley went downstairs to start it over. She pulled Fred so he stood on his hind legs, and we twisted with Fred. We twisted around the refrigerator and on the dining room table.

Then we collapsed on the couch, breathing hard. I promised myself we'd clean up all the mud in the morning. I felt bad about the fluffy snow-white bedspread. Hopefully the powder fresh dryer sheets would erase the mud and make it sparkle.

"I'm making something to eat," Graham said. "You slugs want anything?"

Ashley dropped her head into her hands. "I'm getting one of my headaches."

"What does that mean?" I asked.

"It hurts. It's gonna get worse. I can tell."

Graham looked at me and mouthed, "Now what?"

"Go see if she's got pills in her suitcase," I whispered, so my voice wouldn't hurt her head even more.

Ashley looked at me. "You're really bossy, you know that?"

I could tell she was hurting—her eyes were glassy and red—so I didn't argue. I didn't know if a brain injury headache was like a headache from too much vodka. Aspirin, water, coffee, and greasy food help a vodka headache.

Graham shook a bottle in front of her face. "Is this it?"

Ashley squinted. "I think so."

"How many do you take?"

"It's on the white sheet taped by the sink," Ashley said.

Graham sighed. "We're not at your apartment. There's no sheet."

I took the bottle and read the label. "I can't pronounce it, but it says to take one every six hours as needed. I guess it's needed, huh?"

Ashley swallowed the pill and curled up on the couch with Fred. "Will you rub my temples?" she asked. With her head on my lap, I rubbed circles. Her wig shifted, revealing tufts of hair and patches of scars. On the top of her forehead, there wasn't a scar, really, but a small indent. If she lay straight on her back, you could put a marble in that indent, and the marble wouldn't roll away.

"That's nice, Daffodil. You're so lovely."

"So are you, Ashley."

She smiled, eyes closed.

Graham came back with marshmallows and fat pretzel sticks. I rounded up pillows and blankets for beds while Graham turned off the lights. Then we mowed through the food while Ashley slept.

"Who invented the pretzel?" Graham wondered. "Stupid snack. Flour and salt. And it doesn't even have salt, but salt *pellets*! Who goes to a store, walks past the chips and cheese balls and cookies and thinks, 'Can't wait to get me some pretzels!' "

"People who sell beer," I said. "At the Rattlesnake you get mountains of pretzels. The Chemist says you get thirsty and drink more beer."

Ashley lifted her head and said with a scratchy voice, "You shouldn't have to pay water bills.

Water's everywhere. It should be free." Then she closed her eyes, like she'd been sleep talking.

As we settled into our indoor campground, Fred ate marshmallows and pretzels and Graham counted money.

"I'm not sure he should be eating that stuff. He must have dog food in the barn," I said. "Where are those Beefy Bits?"

"You screwed me up. Now I gotta start over. One, two . . ."

I took the bags from Fred, but man, dogs eat fast. The marshmallows were *gone*. I slid the pretzel bag under the sofa because I was too tired to go to the kitchen. I crawled under my blanket again. I thought about Mom and the Chemist. Who would I miss most? I figured the answer didn't matter, because the Chemist needed *help*. Mom didn't. At least she had Alex, even though he was old and had a ring of hair. Alex told her things like, she's smart enough to get through nursing school, she deserves a good job, and he's proud of her. Which is way better than old boyfriends who said stuff like, "Can you make some tacos, babe?"

So the answer was pretty easy. The Chemist.

And I really missed the Chemist. I missed how we'd sing together back when he had me for sleepover custody. He'd tuck me into the couch and we'd sing "Two of Us" until I couldn't keep my eyes open.

"So what's the plan tomorrow?" Graham yackity-yacked right over my memory.

"Get our clothes. Fill up the trunk with towels and sheets and food."

"We should bring Fred and one of the horses."

"Fred's exactly what we need for the distraction. But a horse? In a car? How's that going to happen?"

"Listen. A storm led us to an empty house with *horses*. We need a crazy distraction for the plan to work, and here we are in this nice house with a barn and three horses. It's a sign."

"Could be one of those weird timing things," I said.

"We need a distraction and a good one. Something that will stop people and make them stare at me instead of staring at you, the illegal person. When they see me, well, I'm a kid on a horse being chased by a vicious dog. A kid who falls off the horse in an explosion of ketchup blood. They won't even notice the Chemist is wire cutting the top of the fence."

"What's wrong with you having a pretend seizure? That's way simpler."

"I don't know what a seizure looks like!"

"Nice time to inform me of that little detail!" I punched my pillow. "Graham, did the Idea Coin tell you this?"

He shrugged.

"Well?"

"I sure wish we hadn't tipped over the refrigerator. We could've made pancakes for breakfast. Or eggs. Or egg salad."

"Answer me!"

He nodded. "Right. The Idea Coin."

Still, if there was no seizure, I thought Fred

chasing Graham was distraction enough. All we needed were the Beefy Bits, and the chase would be on. It was simple.

Ashley breathed soft little snores.

Graham turned off the light.

"Hey," I said. "Will you give me my backpack? It's right by Ashley. Don't wake her up."

I pulled the book from the pack. It was small and pink. The cover had a black outline of a big hand holding a little hand.

"What's that?"

I showed him the cover.

"*Daddies and Daughters: Stories to Inspire and Nurture.* Sounds snoring-boring."

I whispered, "It's supposed to help me remember good times with the Chemist."

"I guess it's cool the Chemist gave you that. I mean, it's all pink and boring and I wouldn't want it, but you know, at least he knew you'd want something like that."

"Go to sleep, Graham. I just want to read something short."

"Read it to me."

"It's private," I said.

"C'mon. I don't have a dad who writes to me. I don't have a dad at all. Read it."

"Your dad might send you things if he knew you existed. He'd probably take you to baseball games and send you checks every week. It's not his fault he doesn't know about you. It's your mom's fault. She shouldn't have dates with men she doesn't know anything about."

Graham snorted. "Thanks, Dr. Daisy. Just read it."

"Fine." I sat up so the moonlight lit up the page. "I like looking at a few pages, in bed, when it's dark. Not when it's quiet because River Estates is never quiet."

"Right," Graham said. "Roaring car engines, slamming doors, blaring TVs."

"Don't forget the drunks," I said. "But don't you get used to the sounds? Eventually all that noise kind of rocks me to sleep."

"I run a fan. Tunes it out pretty nice." Graham shifted closer to me and the book.

I showed Graham the writing on the inside cover. Then I read it.

> A special quote just for you: "Any man can be a father. It takes someone special to be a dad." Your dad is gone for a while but never forgotten. Hang on to your memories, buddy.

Graham took the book and squinted at the signature. He said, "It's not from the Chemist! It says, *Sincerely, Alex.*"

Graham flopped on his back. "So you've got two dads. What do you have to complain about? Give Alex to my mom. I'd take a stepdad like that."

"If you like being left with a neighbor while he runs off to Mexico with your mom."

My eyes squinted, and the words blurred. From my head to my toes, I was tired, more tired than I'd ever been. I yawned. "Just put it away. I'm so tired."

"I will. I'm just gonna look at it for a while," Graham whispered.

The pillow felt like a feather cradle. I sniffed the blanket. It smelled like the laundry sheets in the Powder Fresh box. Nice. Warm.

I hoped the world outside the River Estates Mobile Home Park glimmered and smelled Powder Fresh. In that world, every kid would know their dad and the Rattlesnake Bar and Grill would be the Rattlesnake Carnival. I slipped into the dream, the big beautiful dream, when Graham ripped a long rumbling fart.

He laughed. I laughed, too. We giggled until Ashley lifted her head and asked what was so funny and would we please stop.

Finally I closed my eyes, Graham on one side of me, still looking at my *Daddies and Daughters* book, and Ashley on the couch. I liked the three of us.

My mind swirled right through the tired part. What if tomorrow was a failure—it wouldn't be, but if it was—would there still be a three of us?

THE THIRD PART

DEAR JUDGE HENRY,

I will tell you three things about waking up to the sound of barking and puking.

Number one: When marshmallows return from a dog's stomach, they come up slimy and *whole*. Not one single tooth mark.

Number two: Dog puke is slippery. Graham learned that when he looked out the window near Fred, who was barking and heaving on the floor. Graham landed flat on his back in marshmallow puke.

Number three: When Fred barks and growls and the hairs on the back of his neck stand up and he jumps at the door, it's his way of saying, "Holy crap. There's a guy outside."

In fact, it was also Graham's way of saying it. From the floor he shouted, "Holy crap! There's a guy outside!" A car door slammed. I belly-crawled to the other side of the couch and peeked through the curtain.

Not only was he a guy, he was a teenage guy. He walked around the escape car, checking it out. The back door was still wide open. He picked out the wet map, which fell apart in his hand.

"Wake up." I threw a pillow at Ashley's head.

Her eyes popped open. "I'm awake." She sat up, and her blond-and-pink wig shifted to the side of her head. A few brown hairs slipped out of the wig.

Graham made a face. "Man, this is gross."

"I don't think he lives here," I said. "There aren't any boy rooms upstairs. Everything's all quilted and flowery and old."

"So what's he doing here?"

Ashley and Graham scooted by me and crouched down. The guy wore a baseball cap and a hoodie. Tall and skinny, he crossed the driveway in a couple strides and disappeared inside the barn.

Fred was licking the puke off Graham's back.

I slapped him. "Stop it! Fred, you're disgusting!"

"What are we gonna do?" Graham asked.

I grabbed our backpacks.

"He's leaving the barn," Graham said.

Fred growled. He put his head under the curtain and barked.

"Is he going to his car?" I asked. *Please, please, please let the answer be yes.*

Graham whirled around. "I can't tell. The pickup's in the way." The longest ten seconds in my life followed. "He's coming to the house! Run! Hide!"

We jumped up and froze, waiting for someone to take the lead.

"Upstairs!" I led Ashley and Graham to the bathroom. I pushed the shower curtain open, and we climbed inside the tub and closed the curtain. Ashley reached past the curtain and pulled the fancy guest towel into the shower. She wrapped it around her eyes. Her breathing came hard and fast.

I looked around for something we could use as a weapon. All I could find was shaving cream, so I picked it up and put my finger on the button in case I needed to spray a face. I held a pink razor in my other hand. Graham had the toilet plunger.

My heart throbbed and banged in my ears. The thumping was so loud I was afraid it echoed in the shower. Graham was so nervous he breathed in and out through his mouth, not his nose. Slimy marshmallows clung to his shirt. Man, it was the stink of all stinks! Dog puke and morning breath trapped behind a plastic shower curtain.

We listened. A door slammed, and the killer barking turned into hello barking.

"Maybe he's a robber," Ashley whispered.

"I don't think so," I whispered. "He looked at your car like he knew it didn't belong here."

There were footsteps across the creaky wood floors on the main level. Back and forth. Back and forth. And the clinking of Fred's toenails. Back and forth. Back and forth.

Then a voice. Were there two people? Couldn't be. I figured he was on his cell.

When he stood under the vent, we could hear him. "Mom, it's like somebody partied hard, but there ain't any bottles. No keg . . . Lillian never lets the dog in the house, right? He's in the house! . . . Marv promised me forty dollars, and it's not here . . . I *am* looking around, Mom . . . If he did crap on the floor, I'm not cleaning it up, that's not what I signed up for . . . Man, it reeks in here . . ."

Then his voice got louder. "Yeah, it could be a burglary, but I don't see anything missing . . . I mean, I'm not even sure what they had . . . nobody wants those stupid old records, Mom . . ."

The words faded. My breathing came easier until I heard those clinky toenails outside the bathroom. The door swung open, the shower curtain rustled, and Fred's nose poked through. He was happy to see us. His tail thumped, thumped, thumped against the door.

"Go away!" Graham hissed. "Get outta here!"

"Is it Fred?" Ashley smiled. "Hi, Fred."

"Get!" I pushed his face and pulled the shower curtain shut. In two seconds, his nose was back in the tub, sniffing. *Thump, thump, thump* went his tail.

"Hi, sweetie," Ashley whispered.

I heard footsteps on the stairs and the boy's voice. ". . . Maybe some kids turned it into their party house . . . Of course it wasn't the storm, Mom, that's just stupid."

Then he was close. In-the-door close.

"Get outta there!" he ordered, and Fred barked at him. "Stupid dog." The door closed, and Fred whined from the hall. "I think you should call Marv and Lillian. See what they want to do. I'm just supposed to clean and feed 'em, not solve some mystery."

Then the worst of the worst happened. His jeans unzipped and he started to *pee*. Graham swallowed giggles, and his face turned pink and then red.

"I guess I'd call 911." The pee stopped and started again. "I'm not paranoid. Jeez . . . Okay, I'll hang on." Then he peed some *more*. And thank God for that peeing noise because Graham's shakes were turning into quiet little snorts. I threatened to spray his face with the shaving cream. "What'd Dad say? . . . It's stupid for him to come look at the place when I just told you everything." The toilet flushed. "Damn, it smells. I think the dog barfed and I am *not* cleaning up dog barf . . . So what'd Dad say? . . . Whatever. Tell Dad I'll get him at the office and bring him here so he can see for himself. But I don't got all day."

The bathroom door opened and closed, and I heard Fred's toenails follow the guy down the stairs.

"He didn't wash his hands," Ashley said. It was the world's loudest whisper.

I got in her face. "Quiet!"

Graham couldn't hold back any longer. He buried his face against Ashley's shoulder to stifle the giggles. I smacked his arm, which caused me to drop the shaving cream with a huge thud.

"Now *that* was loud," Ashley said.

And it scared them enough to quit giggling. It seemed like an eternity, but the car engine started, and he rumbled away.

"Did you hear that ginormous leak?" Graham screeched. "I tried timing it but it was so funny I lost count." He snorted and cleared his throat. "That had to be a record. Thank God he didn't take a dump."

"We're screwed," I said. "We're absolutely, completely screwed."

"There's only one thing we can do," Graham said.

"What?"

"Get the hell outta here." He ripped back the shower curtain. "Go!"

We stumbled out of the tub. I grabbed some towels and toothpaste from the cupboard. "Ashley," I yelled. "Go get all the food you can find. Load it in the car! Graham! Get those sheets and pillows. Go in the garage and see if there's extra gas."

"You *are* bossy," Ashley said.

"Daisy, *you* get the sheets and pillows," Graham said. "I'm getting Honey."

"Honey?"

"The horse needs a name, too. And that's all I got. Honey," Graham said. "Just go!"

"Graham, maybe the Idea Coin doesn't get everything right. We don't know anything about horses, big or little."

"I do. I watch cowboy movies. I read horse books."

"Horse?" Ashley mumbled.

"I need Honey," Graham said. "Now I'm sure it's going to work."

I threw my arms in the air. "You weren't sure before?"

"Um, I was pretty sure. Now I'm really sure." Then Graham ran outside. Debate over.

There wasn't time for me to chase him down. So we raced in different directions. Graham was outside. Ashley dropped the towel and followed me to the kitchen. I tossed a paper bag at her and grabbed a plastic one for myself.

Ashley stood at the pantry and stacked cans of soup in the bag. "Do you like cream of mushroom? Because I don't like cream of mushroom."

"Who cares! Just move it!" I yelled. I dug through every drawer looking for money. I found a few dollars and lots of change. And a checkbook. I stared at it a moment. Well, they *were* animal abusers, and this was a desperate time. I put the checkbook in the plastic bag with the money I'd found.

Then I put it together: The church people weren't animal abusers. The forty dollars was for that guy to care for the animals until they got home.

Man, oh, man. We needed to fix the farmhouse mess for the church people who loved their animals. I wanted to clean up—cross my heart and hope to die—but a bomb was ticking.

Forward. We could only go forward.

I swear, Judge Henry, it was like you said when you frowned with those thick eyebrows. I needed to be accountable. I promised myself we'd send them a letter and a check when we were safe. A big check, too, not one that only covered the cost of the mess. At least an extra thirty dollars.

I whirled around to yell at Ashley to hurry, but she'd taken her bags to the car. I dug around for more stuff.

The porch door opened. "Daisy!" Ashley yelled. "Daisy!"

"What?"

"The car won't start. Graham says the battery's dead."

DEAR JUDGE HENRY,

Was it because we left the car door open too long? Was it because Graham turned on the dome light while he read the map? Or was it a Universal Force telling us to *stop*!

You called this moment a "crossroads." I thought you meant an intersection, but the dictionary says *crossroads* is a moment of decision. You're right—we had to make a decision—but you're wrong about it being careless and irresponsible. And that's not back talk. It's respect talk.

There's a point you can't turn back. The Graham Cracker Plot was wired into my brain. I told the Universal Force we had to *go* because I didn't want the County back in our business. I was afraid to go back to school. Kids would find out and call me Crazy Daisy. And if Jesse Ellman picked on Graham, I didn't know whether I'd look at the sky or whether I'd tell him to shut his face and leave my friend alone. If I told Jesse to shut up, then Jesse would bully both of us, and nobody would want to be friends with me, either. Graham wouldn't be my after-school friend. He'd be my *only* friend, my *whole-day* friend. I'd go crazy.

I told the Universal Force we had to *go* because I didn't want Ashley living in a house where nobody danced with her. Because I didn't want to live life without the Chemist. Grandma says the Chemist is a bright light in a dark world. I needed his light.

I looked up at the sky and yelled at the Universal Force, "Nice try!" Then I said swear words I promised the Chemist I wouldn't use until high school.

So this was the deal: I was shouting. Fred was standing next to Honey, who'd apparently let Graham remove her from the stall. Fred sniffed Honey's butt while Graham stared at the battery, his hands squeezed into fists.

Then Ashley pulled my arm. "I'm going to change into my clothes. Let me know when you get it figured out."

"Grab our clothes, too!" I said. "They're still in the dryer."

"This ain't fashion show time. It's get-the-hell-out-of-here time!" Graham threw his arms in the air, but his oversized pants started to drop. He caught them at his knees, tugged them up past his tighty-whities to his waist, and tightened the belt.

I covered my eyes. "Eww!"

Graham said, "That guy is coming back with his dad and maybe the police. Am I the only one who gets it?"

"I get it. I get it. Okay. We can't panic. Our moms are goddesses of the dead battery. Crappy cars that never start in the winter? Tires that blow out? And empty bank accounts? Our moms are self-taught mechanics. We can do this."

Graham nodded. "Okay. I'll see what I can find in the garage. You figure out how we're going to get a horse in the escape car."

He ran to the garage. I shouted after him, "We're not. No horse in the escape car!"

Instead, I ran inside to get more stuff. From the

kitchen I heard Ashley giggle. She was holding a Beefy Bit high in the air and Fred was jumping and twirling in circles. "Want a treat? Do you, sweetie?" He whined and jumped. He pawed her leg and barked and barked and barked. "Do you want a treat, sweetie?"

"Yes, Ashley," I yelled. "I think he wants a treat!"

"You're crabby!" She gave Fred his treat, which he swallowed whole, and she threw the bag at me. Hit me right in the face with Beefy Bits. Fred raced to my side while Ashley flounced downstairs to change. I put the treats and Fred's leash with our stuff. He followed me, whining for more.

"Go away, Fred!"

Graham carried a battery charger to the front of the escape car. It was a small box with a long cord to plug into an outlet, and two short cords dangling from the front. One of the short cords had a red clamp, and the other had a black clamp. I've watched people charge my mom's car a bunch of times, so I knew I could do this.

"Where's the outdoor outlet?" Graham asked.

I pointed to the porch. He plugged the charger in and marched it toward the car. He stopped. The electric cord between the outlet and the battery charger was stretched as far as it could go. He couldn't get any closer.

"I think it's okay." I grabbed the red and black clamps. "They'll reach. Just hold the charger."

I stretched those cords as far as I could, but they were one inch from the battery. Just one friggin' inch.

"A little closer," I told Graham.

Graham stepped forward and the whole thing unplugged from the outlet. "Damn!" Graham plopped the charger on the ground and kicked a rock across the driveway.

Think, I told myself. *Think*.

Fred and Honey stood in front of the garage, just watching and flicking their tails. Honey's reddish-brown hair shimmered in the sun, and she tossed her thick mane like she knew she was beautiful. Fred scratched his ear. Then Fred and Honey exchanged glances and both looked at me.

If thought balloons floated over their heads, those balloons would say *Think, Daisy, think!* and *Gimme me a Beefy Bit, would ya?*

The keys were in the engine from yesterday. I sat in the driver's seat and moved the steering wheel stick from the *P* for park to the *N* for neutral.

"What are you doing?" Graham asked.

"Every time our car dies in the road I have to sit behind the wheel and put it in neutral, and Mom pushes the car to the shoulder. We can push it closer to the outlet. So push! Just a couple of inches."

Graham pushed. He groaned and grunted, but the escape car didn't move.

"The grass is slippery. Get out and help. We don't need anyone to steer."

I pushed, too. I pushed so hard I grunted. My feet kept slipping, and the escape car wouldn't move.

Ashley twirled on the porch. She had on a long black wig, black pants, a tight black shirt, and a black scarf. "This place is so perfect! It's my escape. I wish we could stay."

I yelled, "The Chemist, Ashley. Then we're done."

"The Chemist." She smiled. "The Beatles man."

"Ashley, help us push!" Graham said.

"I don't want to get all muddy."

"We're a team, Ashley," I said. "We need you."

The three of us stood side-by-side, hands on the trunk. We pushed and pushed and pushed, then stopped in panic at the same moment.

We all heard it. An approaching car. Tires crunching on the gravel road. I couldn't see anything through the hedges, but it sounded closer. And closer. And closer. *Please don't let it be a cop*, I thought, *And if it is a cop, please make him fat and slow like Aaron the guard.*

We froze. Fred growled. Honey scraped her hoof on the driveway.

A blue car emerged from the hedges and drove past the driveway. Tires crunched more gravel, and then it was quiet.

Our luck was changing.

"I'm glad it wasn't that boy," Ashley said. "I

don't think we would've had time to get back in the tub."

Graham said, "Okay. False alarm, but the next one might be the cops." He wiped his forehead sweat on his sleeve. "All we need is to move a couple inches. Just get the cord to the outlet. Then stop. If we go too far, we'll crunch the porch. Okay?" We put our hands on the trunk. Graham continued, "On the count of three, give it all you got. On the count of three, push as hard as you can and scream something you hate. Hands on the car. Just push and scream. Something you hate. One . . . two . . . three . . ."

"SCHOOL!"

"PRISON!"

"FAKES!"

Only I wasn't the one who said "prison." That was Ashley.

Then the escape car moved, just a little at first before lurching ahead. Before I could smile, I heard the sound of plastic and metal crunching.

DEAR JUDGE HENRY,

It was the worst sound of my life, the sound of the escape car crushing the battery charger we'd left in the grass. You could call it another crossroads.

Graham's face turned red, and he kicked the crushed battery charger through the grass. A piece of the charger broke off and landed on the porch steps. All we'd managed to do is get closer to the porch, so close that if we pushed again, we'd probably put the nose of the car into the steps. I couldn't find anything to kick, or I would have kicked, too. Ashley flopped down on the porch and buried her face in her hands.

Then a bolt of energy hit me. "Graham! The Idea Coin! Get it out!"

He shook his head. "No, it's not the right time."

"Are you out of your mind? Unless a helicopter drops from the clouds and flies us to Club Fed, this is the time. *This* is the time." Then panic punched my insides. His face looked weird. "Did you lose it? Graham, I told—"

"I didn't lose it!" He put his hand in his pocket. "It's here. It's just that we've been sucking too much energy. We're going to need it when we get to Club Fed. We can't waste it now."

"We won't get to Club Fed if we don't use it!" I yelled. "I swear to God I will punch your face!"

"Too bad we don't have truck keys." Ashley sighed.

"And how would that help?" My voice was snappy. "We don't have a truck."

She said, "The pickup truck right there. In the driveway."

"I know there's a pickup truck in the driveway. But it's not ours and we don't have keys!"

She said, "Too bad none of those keys hanging in the kitchen work on this truck."

Graham tilted his head. Of course. Between the door and where the refrigerator once stood were those church signs and a key rack. I shrieked, "Saints are sinners who keep on going. Thank you, church people!" I dashed into the kitchen and snagged all the keys off the board and met Graham and Ashley at the truck. Graham had both doors open and was already hauling our stash from the escape car to the back of the pickup. Fred jumped into the front seat. Honey just stared.

I put in key after key, trying to get the engine to purr. Fred breathed in my face. He smelled so bad I almost puked on the steering wheel. I shoved him away. Ashley hugged Fred and said, "You're mean, Daisy. And I don't know how to drive a truck."

"Sure you do!" Graham dumped another bag into the back of the pickup. Cans of soup rolled everywhere. "It's exactly like driving a car."

"But it's not a car. It's a truck."

Vrooom.

"I found the key!" I shrieked.

"Same thing!" Graham said. "Steering wheel. Gas pedal. Steer. Push. You won't get into trouble. I swear. I cross-my-heart swear."

"It's so big," she said.

I hugged Fred and told her, "He wants to go,

too, Ashley. Fred's part of our family now. You, me, Graham, the Chemist, and Fred."

Ashley smiled and blew me a kiss.

We had one final problem. Graham insisted we needed Honey, the whole it's-a-sign thing.

"What if it's a sign for something else? Like a sign to leave the horse here."

Graham had never looked so serious. "It's fate. Put it together. Me needing a horse in Canada. Then we find a horse. Me talking about cinnamon bread with honey. Then what did I name the horse? HONEY."

Graham had finished transferring everything from the escape car to the escape truck, and Ashley was behind the wheel, but Graham wouldn't let us leave. "Horses help in all the old escape movies. It's meant to be."

"Graham! Think about it. How are we going to get Honey in the back of the truck? We can't lift her."

"Why not? She's a mini. She can't weigh much."

Honey stared at us and swished her tail.

I asked, "What if she bites?"

"What if she poops?" Ashley wondered.

"We don't have time, Graham. Please. Put Honey back in the barn. We're going to get caught, and it'll be all your fault."

He sighed. "Fine." He led Honey with a rope to the barn. I think Honey was relieved.

A minute later, Graham came back from the barn, straining to carry a long board while leading Honey with the rope.

"What are you doing?" I yelled. "Leave her in the barn!"

"Hold your horses! I got an idea." He grinned at me. "Did you get it? Hold your horses?!"

Ashley laughed. I crossed my arms and shook my head.

I heard the pickup's hatch drop. He was using the board as a ramp. Like Honey was going to happily gallop into the back of the truck? Hah.

"Fine!" Graham shouted. "Don't help. Whatever. I can lift this board and handle a horse all by myself. It's not heavy at all. You just sit there and look pretty, Queens Ashley and Daisy."

I put my hands over my eyes, because I didn't want to watch Graham's disaster when it happened. I heard the board thump somewhere on the pickup. Ashley started reporting to me.

"He's got the wood up like a ramp," she said. "He's tugging on Honey. And Honey is walking up the ramp . . . We're ready to go!" She clapped.

"Done and *done*!" Graham called.

I looked out my window as he dragged the board back to the barn. Seriously, he could be so stupid. I yelled after him, "Hey, cowboy, I'm just sitting here looking pretty and all and I was wondering how you're gonna get that horse back on the ground without that board. But you've figured that out, right?"

He looked at me, all puzzled and confused. Finally I said, "Duh! Horse whisperer, bring the board."

DEAR JUDGE HENRY,

Ashley braked at the end of the driveway, looking both ways for cars. Another pickup was heading down the gravel road. Ashley suddenly seemed to understand the situation—the oncoming pickup truck had a destination, and that destination could be *here*.

She looked at me with huge eyes. "What? What should we do?"

"Pull out naturally. Don't—"

The tires spun in the gravel, and our truck leaped out of the driveway and sped away from the farmhouse, away from the other pickup.

I'd planned to say "Don't spin the tires, don't leap into the road, and don't speed," but it was done. Graham and I turned around and watched the pickup. It didn't turn into the farmhouse driveway. I let out a sigh.

"What if they follow us?" Graham whispered.

"Thanks," I said with an eye-roll. "I actually had two seconds of not freaking out."

"Well, what if they do?"

Just then, the pickup made a right turn and disappeared behind the trees.

We sighed at the exact same time. "Ashley," Graham said. "I thought you were afraid of speeding. Slow down!"

"That was before we were being chased by a pickup." Ashley stared straight ahead.

"Slow down," Graham said again, calmly. "The gravel is going to toss us around and we could end up in the ditch."

"Okay, okay." Ashley breathed deeply. "Slowing down, slowing down." She shook her hair, like it cleared her head. "But I have a question."

"What?" Graham said.

"Where are we?"

Graham looked at me. I shrugged.

* * *

We followed the only plan we had. Ashley announced her new gift of listening to the universe. The universe apparently told her to drive randomly, turning here and there, and there and here.

And it actually worked. I spotted the county road with the two silos and the pine trees. Grandma and I passed those silos on our trips. I knew where we were, and I guided us to the Club Fed neighborhood while Ashley smiled and chatted about the universe.

We parked two blocks from Club Fed on a street with big shade trees. It was turning into a nice spring day—warm and sunny with the smell of new flowers. My heart felt bigger than the sky. Today, the Chemist would be free.

Thanks to the morning's human alarm, aka the teenage boy, we were early. We could break out the Chemist after lunch. But I wasn't sure if we were ready. Every few minutes, I could feel my back and neck tighten. The worries were not just in my brain, they were in my body.

I got the red *Graham Cracker Plot* notebook with the map of the prison and showed it to Ashley. She had studied it the day before, but she didn't remember things like a normal person.

"I'm starving," Graham said. We were packed in the cab: Ashley, Fred, me, Graham. "We could eat right here. There's lots of pretzels in the back." Graham and Fred got out to stretch and dig up some food from the back of the truck. The church people's truck looked even bigger now that we were in town. A farm pickup, big enough to haul big farm stuff. Grandma always complained about the slow farm pickups during our trips. She'd speed past them in her tiny car.

I told Ashley, "Graham and I better change into our clothes first. You got them, right? From the clothes dryer?"

"Nope. I forgot." Ashley delivered this news without regret or shame, or even the common sense of an *oops*. I did not want to scream at that woman, because she was going to be my stepmom, so I stuffed my anger deep in my chest.

"Whatever. I've got this awesome pink granny nightgown. Who needs jeans?"

Ashley said, "I rock this goth look, don't I? The boots make me look all thin and tall. The black jeans, the black tank. My awesome black hair. It's my escape wardrobe." Ashley took a tube of lipstick from her purse and spread it across her lips. The lipstick was dark, almost purple.

"Ashley, you look amazing. You really do. But you don't exactly blend in. I like your chain belt and all, but it's the middle of a sunny day."

"Am I supposed to wear *yellow*? Would that say, 'Hey, boys, check me out. I'm here to save you,'" she said. "That's just stupid."

"We're here to save one guy. The Chemist. Don't talk to anybody else. Don't look at anybody else."

Ashley looked away from me, at the houses on the other side of the street. "Why don't we just go to Canada now? We've already escaped. I don't want to screw up and end up back in my crappy apartment and crappy part-time job. We're already free, my lovely flower girl."

"We're free when the Chemist is free. Don't screw up," I said.

The tone in my voice made her stop talking.

* * *

We'd parked in front of a pretty blue house with white shutters. It was two blocks from a *prison* and still nicer than any trailer at River Estates. Grandma said the people in this town didn't fuss much about the prison. When the college closed, the jobs were gone. This town is small and the only jobs left were like waitressing and fixing tractors. A low-security federal prison had paychecks. But those local job-hunters don't know what I know. Low security doesn't protect the people inside. Why don't you tell people that, Judge Henry? Is it because nobody cares about the people inside? I care. Grandma cares. Everyone in that visiting center cares.

If I ran the world, that college campus would've become a water park.

Ashley poked me and pointed. An old man was in the yard, picking a few weeds and admiring his tulips. He looked toward the truck, and his mouth dropped open. There was Fred, hunched up, taking a huge dump on his lawn.

I rolled down the window. "No! Fred! Bad dog!"

Fred looked at the sky and kept on dumping. The man stormed toward us. "Get that mutt out of my yard!"

"I'm sorry!" I yelled. "Fred, stop!"

He looked like he was going to kick Fred, but Fred growled and showed his teeth. The man stopped walking, but not talking.

"Don't you know it's illegal to have a dog wandering around town without a leash?"

I got the leash and a Beefy Bit from the glove compartment. "We have a leash!" I waved it out the window. Graham took the leash and Beefy Bit from me.

"I'm sorry, sir." I've never heard Graham use the word *sir*. He whistled. "Fred! Come here right now!"

Fred wandered through the guy's flowers, stopping to chew a stem. "Fred!" Graham held out a Beefy Bit. Fred plowed through the flowers, kicking up some yellow petals. He leaped at Graham, who managed to get the leash on Fred while he scarfed up the Beefy Bit. Thank you, inventor of the Beefy Bit!

"You better have a bag to clean up that mess!" The man's growl was scarier than Fred's. Scarier than yours, Judge Henry!

Graham opened the truck door and pushed Fred into the truck. "I've got some bags. I'll clean it up."

"Is that a pony in your pickup? What in God's name are you doing with that pony? Who's in charge here?"

The sides of the truck covered the bottom half of Honey's body. I'd been hoping people would think she was one of those big, weird-looking dogs from

Europe. But I guess Honey looked exactly like a tiny horse.

Fred barked as the man walked around the pickup to talk to Ashley. The man said something about the law and leashes and why we were parked there and why we had a pony. At the same time, Ashley yelled something about him not owning the street and he wasn't the boss of us and she was going to call the cops if he didn't back off.

Call the cops? What was she thinking?

Graham tapped the man on the shoulder and held up a plastic grocery bag like a peace gesture. I could see the dark turds in the bottom of the bag.

The man yelled something at Graham and marched toward his house. Graham got into the truck with the bag.

"We gotta find another place to park. Ashley, drive around the block."

I gagged and plugged my nose as Ashley started the truck. As soon as we were moving, Ashley tossed the poop bag into the man's yard.

* * *

We parked one block from the Club Fed cafeteria. I didn't see any fed-mates or guards, not even Aaron. He once told Grandma and me that he walked the grounds during lunch for exercise. He probably just said it to impress my thin-and-trim Grandma.

But the fence—oh man. It was higher than I remembered. A lot higher. Beyond the fence was the prison lawn. It stretched up a hill that went flat and turned into a big cement patio. That's where fed-mates would be smoking, including the Chemist.

"Crap!" Graham said. "I don't think you'll clear the fence with those wire cutters. That's way taller than our practice tree."

"*That's* a prison?" Ashley peeked over the top of her sunglasses. "Where are the lights and guards? Why are there so many buildings?"

We'd gone over the map with Ashley about a million times. I don't know if she was nervous or

just forgetful. So I gave her the red notebook. "Check it out. Again."

"Seriously," Graham said. "You'll never get that wire cutter over the fence."

"I will. I have to."

Ashley tossed the red notebook to me. "I don't get it. Why don't you just cut a hole in the fence?"

Graham shook his head. "A wire cutter couldn't get through the body of the fence. See how the fence is all crisscrossed? That's heavy-duty steel. Doesn't matter how strong you are. You'd need a train. Or dynamite."

"Then why the hell are we throwing wire cutters to the Chemist?" Ashley threw her hands in the air.

I pointed at the top of the fence. "That curly razor wire at the top is thin. It's not heavy at all. But it's so sharp it'd shred his body if he tried to climb it. He can't cut the main fence, but he can cut that razor wire. That's why he needs wire cutters.

"The Chemist can climb that fence in seconds,

even holding wire cutters. Then he'll snip razor wire like it's string and jump over."

Graham nodded proudly. "Then he's in the truck, and we're on the road."

"Oh." That's all Ashley said.

"And I'm the distraction," Graham said. "Daisy's the thrower. And Ashley, you will just hold Fred's leash until I'm ready for him to chase me and Honey." Graham pointed to the right side of the street. "Ashley, it's important. Don't let go of Fred until I'm ready for him to chase me and Honey. Wait until I'm close to the fence. I'll yell, and you throw treats toward me. When he gets closer to me, I drop more treats and I'll be screaming like he's attacking. So it's me, Honey, Fred, and the Beefy Bits." He patted his old-man pants pocket. "And my ketchup-blood for fake blood."

Ashley looked a little foggy. I elbowed her. "You get it? Listen for Graham to yell. Throw dog treats at Graham. Let Fred go after the treats. The Beefy Bits will do all the work. Then all you have to do is get in the pickup and drive to where I'm standing."

"So I have to drive over the curb and side-walk?"

I wanted to shake her. "YES! Because I will be standing by the fence with the Chemist. Drive! To! Me!"

I didn't think she heard me. She just stared at the fence. Graham said, "Ashley? Don't float away on us now."

"I remember these lines." Ashley took off her sunglasses and set them on the dash. She rubbed her eyes. "It's like a poem or a song. So strange. I can't remember my neighbor's name, but these lines never leave. I think the doctors put words in my brain when my skull cracked open. Then they stitched me up and forgot to take out the words."

Ashley's face looked sad. She took a breath and said,

We did not dare to breathe a prayer,
Or to give our anguish scope:

Something was dead in each of us,
And what was dead was Hope.

The creepy jitters got ahold of me. I think they got Graham, too, on account of how he was staring at Ashley.

"Now I understand," Ashley said. "I think those words have been waiting for this very moment. For that fence." She grabbed three tubes of lipstick from her purse and left the truck with a slam.

We watched as she dug through the stuff in back. "Can you explain what's going on?" I asked Graham.

"Can't even guess," Graham said as he checked both pockets one more time for Beefy Bits and the ketchup bottle.

Ashley spread a sheet over the sidewalk behind us, down by the mailbox. She began drawing on the sheet with her lipstick. *What? Why?* I felt a scream coming, so I swallowed hard. It was one of those screams that would shake the ground, so I had to suck it inside and hope I didn't explode.

"I think we're losing Ashley," Graham said. "We need a backup plan."

I slapped the dashboard. "If she just sits there, the cops are going to grab her. They'll get it out of her. She'll tell them all about us hiding out in Canada."

"Maybe she'll forget that part."

"We've got no choice. We need an idea." I held out my hand. "Give me the coin."

"Too risky. We're gonna need it later. The energy is weak!"

I couldn't believe it. He didn't make any sense. "We've been saving it for this moment."

"We'll need it on the road."

"We won't even get on the road if we don't use it now!"

His lips were firm. "We have a plan. It's simple. You at the fence. Me on the horse. Ashley sending Fred after me, then driving to you and the Chemist. Done."

Something seemed wrong. "Graham, give me the coin. Now."

He crossed his arms. I smacked his shoulder.

"Graham, give me the coin!"

"Or what?"

"I will wrestle you to the ground and reach inside those stinky-old-man pockets and take it." He stared at me with the meanest eyes he could make. "You know I can take you down, Graham Cracker! Your arms are toothpicks! I'll break them in two! And I'll spit in your face—the biggest, longest, stringiest lugy you've ever seen!"

He dug in his pocket. "Fine. Screw everything up." He smacked the coin against my forehead, above my left eyebrow.

"Think." Graham sneered. "Hurry up and be brilliant. We have, like, five minutes."

I squirmed. "It doesn't work that way. Get your hand off my head!" I grabbed his arm with one hand and stuck my elbow into his ribs. He gasped, and the coin dropped in my lap. "Owww!" he hollered. "You hurt me!"

"I warned you!"

I picked up the coin. It was shiny. Too shiny. Then I saw the date. "1987? That's not right. Check your other pocket."

When I saw his face, I knew.

I knew he didn't find the Idea Coin.

I knew it didn't roll under the kitchen rug.

I knew the farmhouse had sucked our Idea Coin to somewhere mysterious, maybe in its vents or pipes or its big farmhouse stomach. It was revenge. Revenge for tipping the refrigerator and stealing food and twisting and shouting where we didn't belong.

Graham pretended to find the Idea Coin to make me calm. Graham lied to me.

DEAR JUDGE HENRY,

Have you ever been shocked? Like really shocked? Not electricity shocked, but brain shocked, when your skull squeezes your brain so hard it's about to turn into goop and ooze from your ears. My tight skull wouldn't let my brain feel or think. I could move, but I wasn't feeling or thinking. I was stuck on forward.

"I didn't want to lie about the Idea Coin, but you were so sad." Graham's voice was husky. "And I thought you'd give up."

So tight. Couldn't even frown. I got out of the truck. Graham did, too. In my flowing granny gown, I whipped back my arm and threw the 1987 coin as hard as I could. It clinked against the curb and rolled down the drain.

"Let's hope your aim is that good with the wire cutters," he said.

"Yeah," I said. "Let's hope."

* * *

Then it was time.

I saw the group of fed-mates with orange uni-
forms leave the cafeteria and light cigarettes. My
eyes swept the group for the Chemist. I saw a
thin, tall guy with a crew cut talking to someone
with thick black hair. That tall, thin guy with the
crew cut was the Chemist. I was sure.

I set the wire cutters on the pavement. Not only
did I have to hurl the wire cutters, now I had to
get Fred ready so Graham could ride off with
Honey and fake his big injury. As for the truck,
the Chemist and I would have to run to it. We'd
lose time, but there wasn't another option. Ashley
had lost herself in some art project.

I gave Fred a snuggle and tried to excite him
with a treat. "Wanna Beefy Bit? Wanna Beefy Bit?
Sure you do. Good boy! Good boy!"

I heard Graham clanging around and in a minute he was standing next to the truck with Honey.

"Honey respects me," Graham said. "She followed me off the truck bed, right down the board."

"Ashley," I called. "If you're going to help, we sure could use it now."

She mumbled something and threw a lipstick tube over her shoulder.

"Forget her. We don't have time for her." Graham tried to put his right leg over Honey's back. She was none too happy about it. Her lips snarled back and she bit at him. Meanwhile, Fred whined for the Beefy Bit I'd been teasing him with.

"Hurry up, cowboy!" I said.

"You think it's so easy? It's not."

Graham did a sort of step-leap and got on her back. He smiled. "Now this is a distraction!"

"Then go!"

But Honey wouldn't move, even when he slapped her backside. Even when I pushed her backside. "If she won't walk," I said, "there's no way you'll get her to run."

A woman on a bicycle stopped in the street next to us. She was one of those superbikers with a helmet, gloves, tight shorts, and a little basket with water, sunscreen, and a wallet. "Hey there!" she said. "You're not supposed to ride the little horses. Their backs aren't meant to handle weight. They're show horses. They're pets."

A good idea hit me, so good that someday I'll list my best ideas and this will be number one. Who needed a stupid coin? I pulled Fred with me as I walked to the lady. I asked her, "Are mini-horses slower than bikes?"

She said, "Excuse me?"

I knew the answer: of course she could bike faster than Graham playing cowboy on a mini-horse! This lady was much, much better. Fred wouldn't care *who* he chased as long as he thought he was chasing Beefy Bits.

"Lady, would you turn your bike the other way?"

"Excuse me?"

"Just turn your bike around for a second."

She whirled around so she was facing the prison. "And what does this prove?"

"I think it's going to prove that bikes are faster than mini-horses." I said to Fred, "Wanna treat? Wanna treat?" Then I threw a handful of Beefy Bits into the lady's bike basket and said, "Go get 'em!"

Fred jumped and ripped the leash right out of my hand. He barked and leaped toward the lady teeth first, and man, I'll tell you, that lady can *ride*. And scream. She was louder than barking Fred, his leash still attached, slithering on the street behind him.

Honey wouldn't move, so Graham jumped off and ran after Fred who ran after the lady who biked toward Club Fed. Graham clutched the ketchup in his fist.

I ran for the wire cutters as Ashley scooted past me and climbed to the top of the truck with the sheet.

"Get down!" I yelled. "We need you to drive!"

Ashley pulled each end of the sheet and held it in front of her. Written in huge letters, in three shades of lipstick, was FREE THE CHEMIST.

My heart about exploded from love for that

woman. My skull even loosened a bit. Before I could pick up the cutters, I saw Graham, still following the Beefy Bit parade, accidentally step on Fred's leash. When the leash quit moving, poor Fred's neck wrenched. The dog skidded to a halt, but Graham was still running, trying to get around the leash.

Graham crashed into Fred. He flipped over Fred and took a face-plant in the street. The red stuff on the street was not ketchup. He was pouring blood everywhere. Fred stopped and sniffed him, but that lady kept riding. "Call the police," she screamed at the fed-mates.

"Sure. Let me get my cell phone." Then the guys laughed. That voice was the Chemist.

Judge Henry, Graham's job as distractor worked better than we'd planned. It was *real*. A man fixing a car in his garage ran toward Graham, calling for help.

My turn. I whirled around, facing the fence. And holy crap, there was Ashley, still holding the sheet. Her eyes were clear; Ashley was back!

"Now or never, flower girl." Ashley winked at me.

I ran with the wire cutters. Fast. I *felt* like a blur. What stood between me and the Chemist: the street, a sidewalk, some grass, the fence topped with razor wire, more grass, and the hill where they smoked. And my right arm.

My feet kept going as I lifted the wire cutters. I needed that forward speed to get them over the fence. I closed my eyes and threw so hard my arm almost snapped off and soared with the cutters.

I heard a clink. They weren't supposed to *clink*. They were supposed to *thump* on the ground.

Sure enough. I'd missed. I threw the cutters with a nice arc, but the arc was too short and the fence was too high. The wire cutters were hooked on the fence. On the *outside* of the fence. Unreachable to anyone locked *inside* the fence.

There was no way the Chemist could climb the fence without those wire cutters in his hand. No possible way. The sharp wires at the top would slice him like Christmas ham.

By now, a crowd of neighbors had gathered around Graham, and Fred was barking up a storm.

Another brain shock. No feelings, no thinking. Just forward. Fast-forward.

I ran back to the truck, screaming at Ashley to jump down, which she did. She wouldn't be able to drive. She'd panic. In ten seconds, she'd have that sheet wrapped around her head.

So I got in the driver's seat, buckled up, and shoved the steering wheel stick from *P* for park to *D* for drive. It wasn't a train, or dynamite, which would've worked better, but where does a girl find cheap dynamite? A speeding farm pickup truck was all we had left.

The truck charged forward. I don't remember using my foot. It just moved and when I say moved, I mean *raced*.

The truck roared into the street.

The truck staggered over the curb and sped across the grass.

The truck punched a hole through the fence.

Metal screeched and scratched and screamed.

The next thing I knew, I was standing on the grass. I blinked and tried to remember what happened in last few seconds. Fear turned me into stone. Or else I had smacked my head on the steering wheel.

The fence had banged and scratched the truck, but it was still running.

The Chemist raced down the hill toward me. "Daisy? Daisy? What the hell!" He hugged me. "Are you hurt?"

"Get in the truck and drive!" I ordered.

"What the hell are you doing?"

"Escaping! To Canada! You're going to marry Ashley and build solar panels, and then clear your name and get an Internet job. But you gotta hurry."

He looked at the truck with wide eyes. The Chemist's hand shook as he reached toward the door. His fingers stopped an inch from the truck, like an invisible force separated them. His eyes blinked, and he looked lost.

"Hurry!" I said.

The Chemist stared at the truck. But he wouldn't

move. He looked at the sky and a tear fell from his face. He took a big breath, like the air smelled better down by the fence, because it was closer to freedom.

That brain-shock feeling? The tight skull? It squeezed sound from my head. I could see, but I could barely hear. Everything sounded deep and slow and far, far away.

I tugged on the Chemist's arm. He pulled away and punched the truck. He rubbed his fist with his other hand, and leaned his face against the truck like it was a warm shoulder. Then he turned around and slid into the grass. On his knees, he blinked tears and stared at the sky.

Sound came back to my ears. Somebody yelled and then a siren roared.

Was I spinning? Must have been because I saw everything around me. Ashley stood inside the fence, still holding the FREE THE CHEMIST sheet. She held it high and proud, but purple mascara and tears trickled down her face. Graham sat on the sidewalk with neighbors holding a towel on his face. Guards circled the fed-mates who pushed and shoved each other.

The Chemist scrambled to his feet and backed away. I grabbed his hand and pulled, but he snapped his hand from mine. He backed away from *me*. His Daisy girl.

I think I shouted, "Do you want out of here or not? Because I want you out of here!"

The speakers on the building said, "Intruder alert. Begin Code Three Lockdown. Repeat: Intruder alert. Begin Code Three Lockdown."

From the hilltop, Aaron waddle-ran toward us. He yelled something like, "It ain't worth it, Jacob. Just do your damn time—it's not that long. If you run, you'll be hiding forever. The guards are here—don't make any funny moves. Don't make your baby see the ugly stuff."

The Chemist gazed at the blue sky, streaked with spring clouds, and a strange smile spread across his face. I think he whispered, "You are one gutsy kid," but there was so much racket I couldn't tell.

Then another voice: "Get your hands in the air."

Then the same voice: "Stay nice and easy."

A long gun pointed at the Chemist's back. He didn't move, just stared through me.

I've felt shame, felt it sink into my stomach and turn my face red, but I'd never seen it on another face until then. Especially not the Chemist's face. He wouldn't—couldn't—look at my eyes.

The voice repeated: "I said, arms in the air. Nice and slow."

The Chemist put his arms in the air, nice and slow, like the voice said.

"Do not make any sudden moves. We are authorized to fire."

Fire what?

Aaron yelled, "I got the kid."

The guards handcuffed the Chemist, and up the hill they went. From the back, the Chemist looked like all the other fed-mates, just a skinny guy, head hanging low, in an orange uniform.

Aaron got in front of me and blocked my view.

I tried to look past him, but he held my shoulders tight.

"You don't need to see this. C'mon. I'll take you to my office."

"See?" Ashley yelled. "Even hope can't get through that fence! I told you: 'What was dead was Hope.'"

"Who's the crazy person?" Aaron asked.

"My friend."

DEAR JUDGE HENRY,

I got crackers in Aaron's office while we waited for a County person to come for me. My brain shock faded. I looked around at Aaron's big metal desk, a bulletin board with official-looking papers, and shelves with official-looking books.

Aaron gave me a glass of water and sat down. He watched me eat for a minute, then he said, "The cops aren't allowed to talk to you because you're underage. But I'm not a cop. I'm security. What we tell each other stays in this room, okay?"

I pushed another cracker in my mouth and chewed.

"Daisy, what were you thinking? Do you realize a guard could have shot all of you?"

"We almost made it. We got so close." I held back tears. I didn't want Aaron to see me acting like a big baby.

"You sure did."

"We could have been halfway to Canada by now."

"At least to the edge of town," Aaron said. "So, Canada? You know you need a passport to get into Canada?"

"A passport? Really?" Now that was a huge hole in the plan. But the Chemist would've figured a way around it. "Aaron, where are Graham and Ashley?"

"The boy that got hurt? The ambulance took him. And the girl? The one in all black?"

"That's her," I said.

"I think the city police were talking to her."

There was a long pause. I put another cracker in my mouth and chewed and chewed, but I couldn't swallow it. So I spit the mess in a tissue from Aaron's desk.

Aaron put his elbows on his desk and leaned closer. "Daisy, we got a saying here, 'You do the crime, you gotta do the time.'"

"But he didn't do the crime!"

"I got a secret to tell you. Your grandma and I have gone to dinner a few times." He blushed. "We talk a lot. We even use the email. And I keep telling her it's time."

"Time for what?"

"To tell you the truth. And since your mom doesn't know how to do it, and your grandma doesn't know how to do it, I'm going to. Your grandma might not speak to me again, but I know what's right and wrong, and they're wronging you with this silence."

I didn't know his big truth, but his face told me it was bad. I sat as straight as possible, waiting for the punch.

"I know you think everything was an accident—the house blowing up, the firefighter getting hurt, your dad trying to put out the fire. But that's kinda misleading. You know what *misleading* means?"

"Lying?"

"Not quite. It's keeping out some information. You get a nugget of truth, but not the whole story. Your family is misleading you. See, your dad wasn't doing some chemistry experiment. He mixed up a batch of drugs. Real bad drugs that hurt people. He was going to sell those drugs. It's against the law."

"I don't believe you. You're a guard. You're paid to lie about the people here." My voice sounded hoarse.

"Daisy, that's not the way it is. The truth is in the police reports, the court reports, and even the fire department reports. Your dad stepped outside to have a cigarette at the perfect moment. He's a lucky son of a gun. If he'd have stayed in that house, the explosion would've killed him. Yes, he tried to put out the fire, but—"

"But you can't put out that kind of fire with a regular garden hose." I sounded like a robot.

"That's right, Daisy," he said. "That's right."

There wasn't much more to say. We looked at each other—me and my grandma's secret boyfriend, the jelly-belly guard who watches over my father, the secret drug maker.

"You okay?" Aaron asked.

"I'm never calling him the Chemist again. Not ever. To infinity."

THE FINAL PART

DEAR JUDGE HENRY,

Mom knew about the County. She knew about the court. She knew we better start looking like good, responsible kids. She called the church people right away, and three days later, we were headed back to the farm. Mom said it would make us look good to clean their house without being ordered to do it. This, she said, would improve our chances with the judge when we went to juvenile court.

Graham had spent a night at the hospital, but he was fine. Bruised and stitched and missing front teeth, but fine. Ashley had been whisked away by a County worker, but I wasn't surprised to hear that. The County was in charge of Ashley's life.

So Mom drove me, Ashley, and Graham to the church people's house. Their names are Marv and Lillian Gunderson. Mom said to call them Mr. and Mrs. Gunderson so we didn't sound like hillbillies.

Kari didn't come with us. Graham said she had a headache. Mom frowned when he said that, and I wondered if Kari and Mom were best friends anymore.

Nobody talked in the car. Mom had finally calmed down, and none of us needed to hear the yelling again. Let me tell you, I had about ten minutes of "Oh, God, you're home—thank you, Lord—we were so worried, my baby, my sweetheart, my angel." And about ten *hours* of "What were you thinking? You could have been hurt or worse—killed—and this is not shoplifting or cheating in school, it's serious stuff and you are so grounded!"

Ashley didn't have parents to yell at her, but she has to see the head doctor. Mom said the doctor would probably give her new head medicine, and the County would take away her car keys forever.

But that morning, on the way to clean for the church people, Ashley was all smiles and bright eyes. She wore a white sundress. How was she going to clean in that? Her wig had long red curls, and instead of working shoes, she wore sparkly sandals with spike heels.

Graham wore the same old jeans and flannel shirt he wore every weekend. His face was swollen and both eyes were circled in purple bruises. Stitches made a track across his forehead. He lost two teeth when he tripped on the leash and somersaulted over Fred. He couldn't say the letter *s* right. It wath tho annoying!

Everything about him annoyed me. That day at the prison, I didn't have any leftover energy to be mad about the Idea Coin. Now I had energy. If he hadn't hypnotized me with that coin at the play dump, none of it would've happened. None of it.

* * *

Mrs. Gunderson answered the door. She was short with an old-lady belly bulge. Her hair was silver-gray and—here's the coolest thing—her glasses were red! For some reason, this gave me hope. A lady with a church heart and Ashley fashion.

"Welcome! Or should I say 'welcome back'?" Her voice was singsongy but it had an edge, like when Grandma's mad at me, but she doesn't want to show it because grandmas don't yell. Ashley glided inside, hugged Mrs. Gunderson, and kissed her cheek. Ashley stretched out that hug until she'd said everything she wanted to say. "I am so, so sorry, Mrs. Sundergun. You are lovely, like a flower, and so is your house. It was a terrible, terrible turn of events. And I am so, so sorry. We were under terrible pressure, but we were wrong. So, so wrong."

I could so, so tell Ashley was full of crap.

Mrs. Gunderson pried herself loose. "Thank you."

"So, so lovely." Ashley squeezed her hand.

"Well," Mom said. "Let's get started. I didn't bring supplies, just people power, like you asked."

Ashley leaned against the window. "Is that Mr. Sundergun?" A man in a baseball cap was trimming weeds along the old fence by the barn.

Mom tapped her own head and whispered,

"She's not quite right up here." Mrs. Gunderson's mouth formed a big O.

"I'm going to say hello. And apologize." Ashley glided right out the door.

"The police couldn't tell us much about the . . . the . . . offenders. There are so many privacy laws, you know." Mrs. Gunderson tapped her own head and whispered to Mom, "Are all three of them not quite right?"

Mom sighed. "There are many, many days when I'd say yes."

Judge Henry, I think everyone I know is not quite right. Myself included.

* * *

Two hours later, Ashley and Mr. Gunderson were sitting in lawn chairs, drinking lemonade in the shade. Fred sat next to Ashley while she stroked his ears. Mr. Gunderson came to the kitchen twice to get Ashley more ice. I guess her ice was too melty. Then he came back for a blanket because Ashley was chilly. Then he came back for a lemonade refill, with plenty of ice, and some cheese and crackers. His face was not grumpy at all. In fact, he had a smile from a denture commercial. Extra-white and extra-big.

When I got to the window upstairs, I saw Mr. Gunderson had brought Honey out of the barn so Ashley could pet her. I wanted to break the window and throw the bottle of window-cleaning stuff at her.

Graham stood next to me and looked at Ashley's lovefest. "That ith a bunch of crap."

Mom came upstairs and called Graham and me into a huddle. "Speed it up. No breaks. No complaining. When Mrs. Gunderson checks your work, look sorry. Really, really sorry."

"Mom, you should go tell Ashley to get off her butt and help."

"Ith not fair!" Graham said.

Mom thought about that and shook her head. "I'm not her boss or her County case worker. You two dragged her into this mess."

Graham said, "Theth not a kid!"

Mom looked at me to translate.

"He means Ashley's an adult."

"Listen to me. And I mean both of you. Ashley's an adult, but not exactly. Get this over with, and fast. I'm running out of things to say to the church lady and I need a cigarette." Mom had started smoking again when we ran away. "You know, Ashley seems to like Mr. Gunderson. She doesn't have many friends her age. Ashley's very, very lonely."

"First, why is everybody using words twice? It's super, super annoying. And second—"

"There is no second, Daisy Bauer. Get your butt back to work."

Mom went downstairs. I took the church lady's chore list from my pocket. Her writing had big loops and would be pretty if it wasn't listing the things we had to do.

"There's not much left," I said. "The bathroom and their bedroom. Let's do the bathroom and get it over with."

Graham cleaned the toilet and the sink. I scrubbed the bathtub, which was the worst job, worse than a toilet, because it had gunky stuff around the sides. A long hair by the drain made me gag.

Graham washed the bathroom floor while I went to the church people's bedroom. I noticed right away. No sparkly white bedspread. In its place was an ugly brown-and-orange quilt. I sat on the bed and rubbed my fingers on the brown square. Rough. Rough and ugly.

I cried a little. Stupid. Why was I crying? I also cried when I saw the church people had a new refrigerator. I was sniffling a lot. When I peeked at Graham washing the bathroom's small window, I could hear him sniffling, too.

Finally, the church lady—I mean Mrs. Gunderson—called us for lunch. This was the horrible part. Having to look at them. Having to talk to them. Learning they're nice people. Feeling guilt, which burns and squeezes your tummy.

Ashley, Mom, and Mr. Gunderson were already

at the table. Mrs. Gunderson brought out salad, lasagna, and garlic bread. It smelled delicious.

"Don't fill up." Mrs. Gunderson smiled. "I made apple pie this morning."

"You really *are* thurth people," Graham said.

Mr. Gunderson got all serious. "'If you forgive men when they sin against you, your heavenly Father will also forgive you. But if you do not forgive men their sins, your Father will not forgive your sins.' That's from the Bible." He took my hand in his right hand and Ashley's in his left. "Let's pray." Everyone else grabbed a hand, too. I stared at the table because that's how people pray on TV.

"Lord, thank you for the bounty on our table. And thank you, Lord, for sharing your wisdom with these children. Show them your light, and may they always look to you for guidance." He lifted his head. "This is such an unusual moment. Let's all say something we're thankful for."

He looked at *me* first. I had no time to think, and I wanted to say something smart. Mom's frown said "Don't screw this up." All I could think of was, *I'm thankful for being thankful.* I couldn't let those stupid words out.

An idea came slowly, but it was good. And it was true. "I'm thankful for my mom." Mom's eyes lit up, and she mouthed words across the table. *I love you.*

Mrs. Gunderson said, "I'm thankful for the gift of knowing how to forgive as our Lord Jesus forgives us."

Mom said, "I'm thankful our children are safe. I'm thankful they're learning what happens when you screw up."

Ashley said, "I'm thankful for kindness, for joy, and for lemonade. You are both so beautiful, so, so lovely. I wish I had parents as perfect as you."

Mr. Gunderson blushed.

And then there was Graham. Mom pre-shuddered.

"I'm thankful we didn't get thot."

"Excuse me?" Mr. Gunderson said.

Ashley smiled and repeated, "He's thankful we didn't get SHOT."

Everyone was quiet. Mrs. Gunderson said, "Why don't you think of something positive?"

"I'm thankful we're almost done cleaning. You know thomething? We're cleaning roomth we never even went into."

Mom nearly sucked her lips into her mouth. "Graham Hassler, you are rude. Try again."

"Fine! Um . . . I'm thankful the County ith paying for me to go to a private thchool with more dithcipline so I don't have to go back to our dumb thchool and Jethe Ellman."

Suddenly he's going to a new school? He learned that in just three days? His mom must have been planning that for a while. Or did he already have a County worker for something else? He hadn't been in trouble for a long time, far as I knew, not since he shoplifted candy last year. Sometimes you don't know the people you know.

Graham seemed pleased with his answer about private school, but nobody spoke or looked at him. Finally he added, "And I'm thankful for my mom."

* * *

And that, Judge Henry, was our day with the church people. I'm thinking that if they could forgive us, and Jesus could forgive us, maybe you can, too.

DEAR JUDGE HENRY,

I have decided to like Aaron again.

I'm only telling you what happened because Aaron says you don't rule the federal prison system, just the County. You can't punish him for breaking a prison rule. Still, I sure wouldn't mind if you kept this news to yourself.

Aaron let me see the ex-Chemist today, even though he'd lost visiting and phone privileges, even though I was still on the visiting ban. Aaron put the ex-Chemist in a secret room at Club Fed and told Grandma we'd have fifteen minutes.

I'd asked Grandma why she misled me about the ex-Chemist. I borrowed *misled* from Aaron because it's nicer than *lied to me*. Grandma said, "There's no reason to tell a turkey it's almost Thanksgiving." When I asked Mom, she said, "What you don't know can't hurt you."

Those are the dumbest answers I've ever heard.

Judge Henry, you're old and hairy and you growl when you talk, but you never use fake words to make something seem better than it is.

Today I got to ask the ex-Chemist the same question.

Unlike the visiting center, this room looked like a real prison. The walls were cement, and you had to squint on account of the low light. Two metal chairs faced each other. The ex-Chemist sat with his back to the door.

Aaron said, "This will be a copy room in a few weeks. We're remodeling." As if it mattered to us. "Remember. Fifteen minutes. Don't waste it." The door shut. I walked around the ex-Chemist and sat in the other chair. The ex-Chemist looked blank and thin. His hands squeezed the armrests like he was handcuffed to them, only he wasn't.

Fifteen minutes. Not enough time for nice.

"Why did you lie to me?"

Fifteen minutes. Not enough time for waiting. "Why? Answer me."

"You're so young. So young."

"When were you going to tell me? When I was, like, thirty or something?"

He rubbed his forehead. "There wasn't a plan, Daisy. Just day by day. That's how you survive here."

"Bull crap. How do you think I survive out there?" Since he wasn't looking at me, I didn't look at him, either. He stared at one wall. I stared at the other. "And why were you making drugs? This guy came to our school and talked about getting addicted and stealing and once he left his baby in the car while he went to buy drugs. And one time he took drugs and thought he was a time traveler and walked through a window and cut himself all up."

"I wasn't really a dealer. It was quick cash and bad timing. Just quick cash, that's all. It wasn't going to be a career. I was looking for a job, a decent job, you know. I really was."

"If you make drugs, and they're not the pharmacy kind, then you're a drug dealer."

What else was there to say? I twirled my hair

around my finger. Finally he looked at me. I could see his face turn out of the corner of my eye.

"Disappointing you is the worst. Worse than being locked up. And if you decide you don't want to be my daughter anymore . . . I guess I'd understand, but I'd be lost. Like really lost."

His voice shook and he gulped a sob. Tears shined up his cheeks. "I'm losing the best years of my life. I'm losing the best years of *your* life."

"Are these really the best years? Really? Right now? The *best*?"

"In your case, not so much."

Aaron poked his head in the door. "Finish up, okay?"

"I got three things to say." My father cleared his throat. "I'm sorry I got mixed up in drugs. I'm sorry I lied about it being an accident and convinced Grandma and your mom to lie, too.

"When I get out of here, it's going to be different. I swear."

I believed that he believed it. So I nodded.

Then he said, "The third thing—Daisy Bauer,

don't you ever, and I mean ever, do anything that stupid again. Ever."

"Same goes to you. Ever to infinity."

"Deal."

He stood up and held his arms out for a hug. Was he sorry? Really sorry? I stuck out my hand for a handshake. When he shook my hand, I could see that his eyelashes were wet.

Aaron opened the door. "Best I can do, guys. Time to go."

I walked around the ex-Chemist. I needed a hug, so I rushed to Aaron. He didn't look like a guard then. He looked like a big teddy bear waiting for a kid to squeeze his belly. He leaned down, squished me with his big arms, and said, "Six months before you see him again. Six months until another hug."

For a second, I thought, *Six months isn't long enough!* Immediately I started shaking, like someone put a quarter in my back and pushed the cry button. The ex-Chemist was behind me. He pulled me back against his chest. He squeezed me and kissed the top of my head.

"Will you write me lots of letters? Long ones, with lots of detail, so I know everything that's going on with you? Can you do that? Would you?"

"Yes, I can write letters," I said. "Real long letters."

I didn't say anything about my letters to you, Judge Henry. The ex-Chemist thinks all judges are mean and unfair, but he's been wrong about so many things. You *look* mean and unfair, Judge Henry, but I notice you nod when people talk. I think you're really listening. I think you're really reading. I think you're nodding right now.

DEAR JUDGE HENRY,

Your timing stinks! You missed everything in the courtroom today because you had that secret meeting with the County people. We waited and waited while you were "in Chambers," as you called it. Why do you have a Chambers? Isn't that where kings and queens drink tea? I asked Alex about Chambers, and he said it's like your office or something. That's why people are scared of judges. You bang on your desk with a hammer and say weird things like "Chambers" instead of "office" and "juvenile" instead of "kid."

Anyway, while you "chambered," someone lit a fuse and it was dynamite central. Remember the old cartoons where cats and roosters set bombs, fall off cliffs, and hit each other with hammers? That's what happened.

Mom, Alex, Grandma, and me sat in the first bench. Behind us were Kari, Graham, and Ashley, who had on her red wig and bright red lipstick.

She leaned over the bench and hugged me. "Hey there, flower girl," she said. "Hey there, dancing queen," I said.

When you left, Judge Henry, Mom said to Alex, "Chambers? See what the County does with our tax money?" Grandma snorted and said, "The County should use our tax money to teach parenting skills."

BOOM!

Alex told Grandma my mom is a wonderful mom, and Mom told Grandma she raised a crappy son who deserved to be in prison, and Grandma told Alex to mind his own business, and Mom yelled at Kari for being a terrible babysitter, and Kari yelled at Mom because Graham would have never done something so terrible on his own, and Grandma said I'm a wonderful child who's never been in trouble so it's Graham and Ashley's fault, and Kari said leave Ashley out of it because she can't be held responsible.

And on and on it went.

Graham still had stitches in his forehead,

and the color on his face was more green than purple. He motioned me to come to the end of the bench. He said, "Your mom ith blaming everything on me."

"Sounds like your mom is blaming *me*."

"Well, it wath your idea."

My eyes about popped from my face. "My idea? *Me?* Who wanted to go to Canada?"

"Who wanted to break out the Chemith?"

"Who couldn't read a map? Who pushed over the refrigerator? Who stole a pony?"

"Not a pony. A horth. I *borrowed* a horth."

My temper boiled up my insides. "I said everything was messed up, but you—"

"You thaid I was Thuperman and Harry Potter and you hugged me all thupid."

"I would never ever ever call you Superman or Harry Potter. Maybe Stupidman or Harry Snotter. You're too weak and dumb and weird for a superhero."

"Your dad wath too chicken to run! Big dumb chicken!"

In my mind, he didn't mean the ex-Chemist was *chicken*. Graham meant *drug dealer*. I saw it on everyone's face, all day, every day. The checker at the grocery store. The guy who delivered our pizza. Frank the Creeper. I could read their thoughts. Everyone who looked at me was thinking, *She's the daughter of a drug dealer*.

I screamed, "You only wanted to run away so you could have my dad as your own, you freaky dad thief!"

He looked at me, lips pinched, eyes all sad and mad.

I jerked back my fist and just as I was going to wham-bang his head, two arms circled around me and pulled me across the floor. I could tell by the hair on his arms it was Alex. He pulled me toward the door, and the whole time I screamed, "It's all his fault! Graham Cracker! It's his fault!"

Suddenly we were out in the hall. Mom, Alex, and me. Mom didn't even yell. We sat on a bench, and she hugged me and stroked my hair.

Ten minutes later, a guy in a uniform told us to

go home, the judge rescheduled the hearing. Again.

"Why?" Mom asked.

"Who knows?" The uniform guy shrugged. "Maybe the social worker forgot some paperwork. Heck, maybe Judge Henry's getting lunch for a change." He thought about it. "Put your money on the paperwork. The judge never has time to eat."

THE PART WHERE
I'M SUPPOSED TO
WRITE TO YOU

DEAR JUDGE HENRY,

At court last week, you told me to write the letter to you. You want me to explain responsibility and what I've learned and what I'm sorry for. Mom said I'll learn my punishment later.

So I'm writing. I am COOPERATING. It's late at night, and I'm still writing.

At first, I didn't want to write anything. But once I started, everything burst out, like my pen caught fire. The story is burning inside me, and nobody can stop it. Not with a garden hose, not with a fire hose, not with rains from a hurricane.

BACK TO THE
FINAL PART. AGAIN.

DEAR JUDGE HENRY,

The kids at school haven't heard about Club Fed. Here's how I know: Jesse Ellman and gang haven't called me Alcatraz Bauer or Jail Breaker or Crazy Daisy. But they'll find out eventually. Secrets are the only things that escape Club Fed.

Graham doesn't have to worry about Jesse anymore. His new school doesn't let kids mess around—at all! He had his final meeting in court. His punishment is raking leaves for old people this fall and working at the food shelf all winter. And he's on probation, which I think means no more chances. Lucky for Graham, the County paid for him to get fake front teeth.

I wish I knew my punishment. The waiting is making me chew my fingernails, and Grandma won't paint them until they grow out. Just tell me whether I'm raking leaves or whatever. Why are you taking so long? Why can't you just decide?

Mom and Alex think it's because I didn't have

any law trouble before this and you don't want to be too mean but you also don't want to be too nice. Plus Mom said my County person is on her honeymoon and everyone needs her report. Mom sneered when she said that.

Maybe we have the same problem, Judge Henry. You aren't sure if I'm really sorry. Just like I'm not sure if the ex-Chemist is really sorry.

But don't you do this all the time? Aren't you like a lie-detector machine? You're a judge!

Every day, you look at people's eyes and wonder, *Is he really sorry? And that lady . . . is she telling the truth? And him . . . does he really understand he did a bad thing? And him . . . the skinny guy who used to clean carpets, the one with the daughter named Daisy . . . how'd such a great guy turn into a drug dealer?*

And that great guy, the ex-Chemist, did he look into the eyes of his judge, or did he stare at the floor? I wonder. Did his eyes say, *Guess who I was before this. Guess.*

DEAR JUDGE HENRY,

I haven't seen Graham for a long time. Kari drives him to his new school. He doesn't even wave. Just stares straight ahead.

I'm sorry. Two little words. How hard could it be for him to spit 'em out? Mom says I should apologize. I wish Graham would say he's sorry first, because he did the first lie. I think. It's hard to remember exactly. If he said he's sorry, then we could hang out again. He could show me how he pulls out his new front teeth. I've been wondering how he does it.

"You know how many times I told your father I was sorry and never meant it? Trust me, it ain't hard," Mom said as she lit a cigarette. We'd just finished eating hot dogs for dinner, and the taste of ketchup was still in my mouth. How could she cover up that deliciousness with stinky smoke?

I coughed and waved smoke from my face.

"Why'd you do that? If you don't feel sorry, why say it?"

"So he'd shut the hell up," she said.

"I wouldn't do that to Graham."

"Do what?"

"Lie about being sorry."

She rolled her eyes. "Are you sorry? Or not?"

I stared at our dirty, brown carpet. "Everyone at school had been so mean to him for so long. I thought I was okay because I didn't join in. So I feel like a big turd for that." I stopped a second to chew on my thumbnail. "Then, in the courtroom, I said some pretty rotten stuff."

"Does that mean you're sorry?"

"When I think about those mean words and just about Graham being Graham, my stomach flops. There's this whole awful mess, but I guess what I'm most sorry about is Graham. But I don't want to see him because he'll yell at me and say he hates me."

She stared at me, reading my face for something. When she thought she'd found it, she grabbed my shoulders tight. "Don't you dare tell that judge

you're *most* sorry for Graham. I mean it, Daisy.
You tell him what he wants to hear or else. You
tell him you're sorry you broke into a house, you
stole, you vandalized, you caused a prison lockdown!

"If you're sorry about being a rotten friend,
then go talk to the friend. But this judge doesn't
care about your social problems, understand? And
neither do I! I care about you cleaning up your
act! So leave Graham out of it. Apologize for the
damn crimes." Her voice cracked. "*Crimes*. I used
the word *crimes* with my own kid."

I rubbed her back until she stopped crying.
Then I got a wad of toilet paper so she could blow
her nose.

* * *

After school, I knocked on Graham's door. His
face didn't light up like I hoped.

I asked, "Do you want to throw me in hot lava?"

"Kinda."

My arms crossed themselves even though this

was a peace mission. "So you want to see me burn up like a French fry?"

"I'd give you pain medicine so it wouldn't hurt so much."

"Gee, thanks."

"No problem."

I looked over his shoulder. Kari and a woman sat at the table looking through papers. And that woman wore a blazer. The County lady! It had to be. No wonder his mood was bad.

I lowered my voice. "How's your new school?"

"Stupid. A couple guys asked me how I got the forehead scar, and I said I was breaking a friend out of prison and a guard pounded me, and now everyone's afraid of *me* because I'm so tough. No more bullies."

"Now you're the scary one. But no friends, either, right?"

He shrugged. "I'd rather be scary than scared."

That guy cannot catch a break. I took a breath so peace would fill my lungs and I could blow good feelings between us. I said it fast. "I'm sorry."

He nodded.

"And?" I said.

"And what?"

I squinted at him. I told myself, *I'll count to ten and if he doesn't say it, I'm leaving and never speaking to him again. OneTwoThreeFourFive-SixSeven—*

"How come you don't go to the play dump anymore?" he asked.

"Huh?"

"The play dump."

Before I could answer, he jumped off the steps, missing a puddle by an inch or so. He jogged to the play dump and plopped into a swing.

"You can't just walk away!"

Graham yelled, "Just come here, would ya?"

I stared and kicked rocks.

"C'mon, Daisy. Just swing for a while."

So I sat on the other swing and pumped hard to

catch up. Graham dropped his shoulders back and stretched his legs. He looked like he could fall asleep. The apology must have been stuck in his throat.

Whatever. Mom and me were probably moving into Alex's house. I'd live on the other side of town. Once kids stopped being afraid of Graham, he'd make some friends. Maybe his friends would never know his "scholarship" comes from being an at-risk kid. Mom says at-risk means the County's afraid he'll drop out of school and become a thief and an alcoholic or worse. I knew *worse* meant *drug dealer*.

Did the County think Graham would be a fed-mate someday? Graham was a pest and a pain and, sure, we did break the law, but we thought we had a good reason. The Graham I know, the Graham who dreamed about horses and Canada, would never end up in Club Fed. But what about a thirty-year-old Graham who didn't have a job and couldn't pay child support and spent his nights at the Rattlesnake Bar and Grill?

Come to think of it, I was probably an at-risk kid, too. The bad-influence kid. The kid all the parents figured would turn into a drug dealer, like her father, and an alcoholic, like her mother. The kid with a record and I don't mean the Beatles. I mean a record with you, Judge Henry.

That's when I saw it.

In the bottom of the sandless sandbox was a bunch of long, fat pretzels, just like the ones we ate at the farmhouse. Only these were shaped into something. I dug my heel in the sand to slow down. The pretzels formed words. And the words said:

> Sorry Daisy from Graham
> Queen and King
> of River Estates

He stopped swinging, too. "Do you know how many days I've been writing in pretzel? You never come out here after school, and by the morning, it's messed up because raccoons and cats eat it.

Sometimes it's totally gone. Yesterday it was part gone. Yesterday it said: Frog ham kin ates."

I laughed so hard it turned into a cackle.

"I had to buy ten bags of pretzels, Daisy. Ten!"

"Queen and King of the River Estates Mobile Home Park," I said. "It could be worse. We're not going to live here forever like Frank the Creeper. We're only here for temporary."

"Right. We're only here for temporary."

After that, we pumped as high as the swings would take us. Not talking, not joking. Just listening to the squeak-creak of the swings until our moms called us in for dinner.

THE ACTUAL FINAL PART

DEAR JUDGE HENRY,

I think I'm actually going to miss writing to you. You've been a good listener. I bet you're not so scary when you're wearing tan pants and a golf shirt. Maybe you can visit someday and Grandma can cut your hair and wax your brows.

I'm glad the big hearing is over. Finally.

I was listening, in case you were wondering. You said I will spend the summer picking up trash in the parks and pulling weeds on city grounds. Those jobs are exhausting. Who knew the city had so many grounds? I also have to talk-talk-talk to a County lady about my problems. That's going to be worse than picking up garbage!

So this is the part where I write about my feelings and stuff.

The County lady says I should make two columns. One column should be "My Remorses." (Yeah, I had to look it up, too. It means sorrys.) The second column should be "Things I Learned

About Responsibility." Like I told you, my mom says I should just say whatever you want to hear. And Grandma said, "Aren't you done with that thing yet? I've never read a book that long!"

I'm just going to say what's what and that's that. Some of it you won't like, but I want you to know I'm not listening to the County lady or Mom. I wrote all this stuff myself. Nobody helped except the dictionary. I guess you know me by now, Judge Henry. You'll be able to tell if I'm yanking your robe.

So, here goes . . .

I'm *not* sorry I wanted the ex-Chemist to live with us in Canada. But I *am* sorry I tried to break him out of Club Fed. Aaron says we're luckier than hillbilly lottery winners nobody got seriously hurt. I'm already responsible for a list of crimes, and that's heavy enough for my heart. If someone had died, my heart would shrink up and die, too.

I'm *not* sorry for wanting out of the River Estates Mobile Home Park. Alex says dreaming about a new life is fine. It's the *doing* that can make all your troubles. I *am* sorry I did my dreams wrong and hurt people.

Mom says we're lucky you gave us second chances. So thanks for that. I promise to never, ever need a third chance. But why me? Why Graham? Why can't the ex-Chemist have a second chance? I get that we're kids and he's an adult, but you don't learn *everything* before you grow up. You learn until grass grows on your grave. Maybe the ex-Chemist learns slower than most people.

I *am* sorry we broke into the church people's house, stole and destructed their stuff, and twisted and shouted on their sparkly, white bedspread. And I *am* really, really sorry I crashed their truck in the Club Fed fence.

I'm sorry for lots of things. I'm responsible for lots of things. But the worst thing I did, and what I'm most sorry for, is pinning the mess on Graham and shouting all nasty at someone who can't take more nasty shouting. He's a friend. My friend.

Remember when I said if you broke up this story into one million pieces of blame, only two of the pieces would be mine and 999,998 would belong to Graham? That's not true. We were partners. We only called it the Graham Cracker Plot because it sounded cool.

That day at Club Fed, the day the Graham Cracker Plot failed, Ashley told us about this poem she couldn't forget. The poem had something to do with the Club Fed fence and hope dying. When I think about the ex-Chemist being a bad guy in prison, I feel hope leaking out of my body. So I tell myself, the ex-Chemist is a *good* guy in prison. A mostly good guy. A dad who wants to be better at being good. Those thoughts help plug the leak.

Now I have to tell you the Big Truth, bigger than the Graham Sorry. My hand hurts from writing so much truth! But it's important. Mom won't want me to write it, and you won't want to read it, and the County lady won't want me to feel it, but right now I am the Queen of Truth, so cover your eyes if you can't handle it.

I will always love the ex-Chemist.

ONE MORE THING

Dear Ms. Bauer,

I've read each of your letters with great care. I expected one letter, perhaps a long letter, but certainly not several notebooks. Your thoroughness is noted.

The following are answers to your questions you sent along with the notebooks. You didn't need to worry about me losing the paper with the questions, as it was taped, glued, and paper clipped to the first notebook.

1. I wear a robe, not a dress, and yes, I wear pants and a shirt underneath. Judicial robes have a long tradition in the courts. I agree with your grandmother. Black is a slimming color.
2. No. I do not send children to prison.
3. My children are grown up. And no,

they do not think I am mean. Neither
do my grandchildren.

4. Thank you for the offer to wax my
   eyebrows, trim my mustache, dye my
   hair, and have injections in my frown
   lines. I'm sure your grandmother
   is a fine stylist, but judges cannot
   give or accept gifts or services from
   people involved in a case. Besides,
   I think frown lines are distinguished.
   Don't you?

5. My favorite movie is *The Verdict*. I
   suggest you watch it when you are
   much older.

6. Yes. I did get in trouble when I was
   a kid. I took my dad's cigarettes and
   smoked them with friends behind the
   malt shop. My brother squealed
   on me. (That's what we called it
   back then.) My parents wouldn't let
   me go to the school dance. That
   girl who was supposed to be my date,

Barbara Ott, was the prettiest girl in
school. She married the boy who
took my place!

7. Yes. It appears you are on a path of
responsibility and understanding.

8. I also do not like the labels "child at
risk" or "child in need of services."
Such negativity. I think you and your
friend Graham, and hundreds of
other kids, should be called "children
in need of hope."

* * *

Ms. Bauer, I do not want you to give up love or
hope. Love your father, the ex-Chemist; love your
mother; love your grandmother; love your friend
Graham; love your friend Ashley. Love people,
but don't confuse it with loving their behavior.

I'm including with this letter a photograph
of an iris. Judicial ethics forbid me from giving
you anything of substance. In this case, I am in
complete and utter violation of ethics because

nothing is more valuable than an iris. Daisy is a lovely name, of course, but an iris has extraordinary power. An iris is a symbol for hope.

I have great hope for you, Ms. Bauer, hope as big as the sky. The question is, do you? As I envision you reading this letter, it is *my* hope that you are smiling, hanging the iris photo on your bedroom wall, and dreaming of your bright, beautiful future.

Sincerely,
Judge Franklin L. Henry

DEAR JUDGE HENRY,

I will tell you three things right now.

Number one: I smiled.

Number two: I hung the iris photo on my bedroom wall.

Number three: I bought a new red notebook so I'll be ready when the dreams come.

ACKNOWLEDGMENTS

I started writing stories in first grade, so my acknowledgments could exceed this book's length. Therefore, I begin with people who taught me the value of brevity: editor Kathy Vos and professor Michael Norman. I hope they'll understand this lapse, but I'm compelled to note people who influenced me. High school English teacher Mary Louise Olson read my work out loud and announced I had talent. Terry Davis pushed me to grow as a writer and opened his career network to me. My parents, Robert and Karen Grubb, and my sister, Cheryl, applauded career highs and supported me during personal lows. Michael Ott fueled my motivation when it waned. My Sisters in Ink and friends (J. Angelique Johnson, Kirstin Cronn-Mills, Becky Fjelland Davis, Kristin Dodge, Sally Chesterman, and Rachael Hanel) shaped my fiction, including this book. Denise Whiteside Bunkert inspired me to write full time when she made art her career, not a hobby. Nick Healy assigned a nonfiction project that led to my first critical success, *Little Rock Girl 1957: How a Photograph Changed the Fight for Integration*. My godchild Brittany Frary opened my heart to the joy and wonder of childhood. Brynja Johnson and Wendy Tougas, the first kids to read my early work, fostered my confidence. Joe Tougas taught me rejections were accomplishments because I'd joined the small club of writers who actually caught the eyes—if not the contracts—of editors. Mohamed Alsadig offered big hugs during tough times and, to this day, remains Minnesota's most handsome man. Other friends gave me love and laughter: Cherie Richter, Amy Barnett, Dawn Schuett, Wendy McKellips, Diane Winegar, Bruce Lombard, Greg Abbott, Valerie Brouillard and the Brouillard family, Victoria Ott, Sherry Crawford, Sue Munsterman, and Donn Jenson. The Roaring Brook team brought this book into the world. And, finally, my heartfelt thanks to agent Susan Hawk, my publishing partner and champion.

SQUARE FISH

DISCUSSION GUIDE

THE GRAHAM CRACKER PLOT
by Shelley Tougas

Part One

1. After reading the first letter to Judge Henry, create a list of ten questions and ten facts about Daisy. Put a star next to the three that you think will be most important to the story.

2. Describe the Chemist, especially his unique qualities.

3. Explain how Daisy's mom and grandma get along (or not). Why does Daisy have to be careful about what she says?

4. Why does Daisy believe her grandmother wanted her to bust her dad, the Chemist, out of prison? What happened that made her suddenly want to do this crazy thing? Why is the Chemist in prison, according to Daisy?

5. Do you believe in the magic of an idea coin? What is special about Graham's? What happens when Daisy uses it for the first time?

Part Two

1. Describe where Daisy and Graham live. How are their home lives similar? How are they different? What made them become friends in the first place? Is Graham's mom a good babysitter or not? Why?

2. Why do they end up inside a stranger's house instead of at the prison? Make a list of everything they do there that could get them in trouble. Then, rank those actions by the amount of trouble they could get into, starting with the worst. Put a star next to the one that would get you in the most trouble.

3. After an argument, Daisy says, "When you asked me if I had any shame, I tell you, cross my heart and hope to die, my shame then and there almost burst my body into flames." (p. 132) What made her feel like this? Have you ever felt like this because of the way you treated someone?

4. Graham forces Daisy to listen to the voicemail on his phone. Why? What are the pros and cons for going back and forward at this point in the story? Why can't Daisy bring herself to give up on this idea?

5. How do they revise the plan with the new set of circumstances? How are they planning to distract the guards?

Part Three

1. What happened to their escape car? How do they try to solve this problem? In the end, what do they use instead?

2. What is a crossroad? Do you know if a decision is a crossroad as you make it or only after it's over? Which decisions they make are crossroads for Daisy and Graham?

3. Outline the plan to bust out the Chemist step-by-step. Then, discuss in pairs what's most likely to happen. After reading this section, list what actually happened instead.

4. How does Daisy try to save the plan when it is completely falling apart? How does her dad react? What does the guard think about her plan?

5. What's Aaron's definition of misleading? Do you agree with him? Should Daisy have been told the truth about her father from the beginning? What might have been different if she had known?

The Final Part

1. Why was eating with the Gundersons the most difficult part of the day? Think about the way each of them answered for what they are grateful for. What does it tell us about their characters (or what type of person they are)?

2. When Daisy can see her dad for fifteen minutes, how does it go? Would you hug him? Write him? Forgive him if he was your dad?

3. How is the judge deciding about Daisy in the same way she must decide about her own dad? How do you know if someone really regrets a mistake?

4. How are things patched up between Daisy and Graham? How does he finally apologize? Why is it so hard to apologize to people who are important to us? Why does Daisy's mom tell her to handle her friendship and tell the judge what he needs to hear?

5. Predict fifteen years into the future. What will Daisy become as an adult? Do you think she'll be successful or not? What about Graham?

GOFISH

SHELLEY TOUGAS

What did you want to be when you grew up?
A writer. I wrote a picture book in kindergarten, and my best friend illustrated it. It was called "A Robin Lays an Egg." Now I'm a writer,

© Mary Reisdorfer

and she's an artist. We both always knew what we wanted.

What's your most embarrassing childhood memory?
Pretty much every time I played kickball because I was the worst kickball player ever. I couldn't kick, catch, or run fast. I basically lacked every single skill needed for kickball.

What's your favorite childhood memory?
My first plane ride. My grandmother flew my sister and me to a family reunion because we'd never been on a plane. I was six, maybe seven. We dressed in our best clothes, and my mom curled my hair. We got to drink soda during the flight and listen to music with headphones that plugged into the arm rest. We took turns sitting in the window seat. I remember pretending I was in a spaceship.

As a young person, who did you look up to most?

I was a fanatic about President John Kennedy, even though he died before I was born. When I was ten, I could name the members of his cabinet.

What was your favorite thing about school?

Reading and writing. No surprise there. I was pretty stubborn about my reading selections, though. I didn't like being assigned books by my teachers. I wanted to pick out my own.

What were your hobbies as a kid? What are your hobbies now?

I'll skip the part about reading and writing and go right to *Star Wars*. I watched the movies, read the books, played with the toys, joined the fan club, listened to the soundtrack, and collected the trading cards. I saw *The Empire Strikes Back* at least twenty times at my local theater. I still love *Star Wars*—the original trilogy, that is—but now, my hobbies are mostly books, cooking, movies, and family game night.

Did you play sports as a kid?

My horrible kickball skills reflected an overall lack of athletic ability and interest. If riding my bike around the neighborhood counts as sports, then yes, I played sports as a kid.

What was your first job, and what was your "worst" job?

My first job was stuffing ad flyers into newspapers. I was fourteen. We did this by hand every Saturday morning, and I'd be covered in ink by the time I was done. My worst job was working in a small store when I was a teenager. The owner was the world's grumpiest man.

What book is on your nightstand now?
Every Soul a Star by Wendy Mass and *Brown Girl Dreaming* by Jacqueline Woodson.

How did you celebrate publishing your first book?
Nothing crazy. My husband took the day off work and we ate tacos and cupcakes. We went to an indie bookstore in St. Paul and found my book on the shelf and took pictures.

Where do you write your books?
I have a big closet we converted to an office—a "cloffice." But I often write at the dining room table or go to a coffee shop. Sometimes, I write with other writers because I miss having actual coworkers. Writing is a lonely profession.

What sparked your imagination for the idea coin?
When I was a kid and my cousins would visit, sometimes we couldn't think of anything to do. So we created "thinking corners." We'd each huddle in our thinking corner until we got ideas. Then we'd vote on them. I thought about that when I was writing Graham's character, and I changed the corners to a coin.

Why did you write *The Graham Cracker Plot* as a series of letters?
I planned to begin the story with one letter to the judge that would set the stage for the book. The rest of the book was

going to be a straight narrative. I liked the letter so much that I started adding more. It seemed like Daisy took over and demanded her story be told directly to Judge Henry.

What challenges do you face in the writing process, and how do you overcome them?
I'm easily distracted. Sometimes, I actually have to use a timer to stay focused. I set it for thirty minutes and force myself to stay with my manuscript. When it goes off, I stretch, check email, and maybe do some laundry before sitting down for another thirty minutes.

What is your favorite word?
Pizza.

If you could live in any fictional world, what would it be?
I want to copilot the Millennium Falcon and be a Jedi knight. It might be my destiny.

Who is your favorite fictional character?
I recently read *The Book Thief* and fell in love with Liesel Meminger. I admire her determination, insight, and humanity.

What was your favorite book when you were a kid? Do you have a favorite book now?
I read everything Judy Blume wrote. If Judy Blume published a grocery list, I would've saved my allowance, bought the list, and read it repeatedly. These days, I'd say *The Poisonwood Bible* by Barbara Kingsolver is my favorite.

If you could travel in time, where would you go and what would you do?

I'm a worrywart. I'd be afraid to time travel because I could disrupt the space-time continuum and destroy the universe. But if I could be assured of complete and total safety, I'd hang out with suffragettes like Elizabeth Cady Stanton and Julia Ward Howe and join their fight for women's right to vote.

What's the best advice you have ever received about writing?

Carry a small notebook and keep another next to the bed. Ideas are everywhere—the grocery store, the dentist, the movie theater. If you don't write your thoughts down when they strike, they're gone.

What advice do you wish someone had given you when you were younger?

Play more, relax more, sleep more, laugh more.

Do you ever get writer's block? What do you do to get back on track?

When I feel blocked, I take a nap. That strange place between being fully awake and fully asleep is rich with creativity.

What do you want readers to remember about your books?

That they had heart and humor.

What would you do if you ever stopped writing?
I think I'd become a nurse. The stories from that job would be amazing.

If you were a superhero, what would your superpower be?
Clearly, I'd be a Jedi knight and defeat the dark side of the Force through my outstanding use of the lightsaber.

Do you have any strange or funny habits? Did you when you were a kid?
When I eat cereal, I crush the flakes with the back of my spoon until I have a mound of cereal dust. Then I pour in the milk. I developed the technique as a kid, and it's still the only way I can eat cereal.

What do you consider to be your greatest accomplishment?
I decided I wanted to publish a novel, and I worked toward that dream despite many, many setbacks and obstacles. I didn't quit, even though I considered it. There were times when I wanted to throw my laptop out a window and watch it smash into pieces. I'm proud I didn't give up.

What would your readers be most surprised to learn about you?
That I am always in possession of seriously overdue library books. I'm surprised they haven't confiscated my card. My library could stock a new wing with my fines.

GET READY FOR A BRAND-NEW MYSTERY ABOUT TWO
FRIENDS, AL CAPONE, AND A PILE OF LOOT.

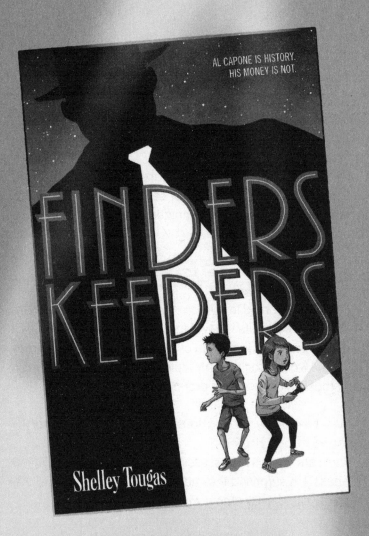

AL CAPONE IS HISTORY.
HIS MONEY IS NOT.

FINDERS
KEEPERS

Shelley Tougas

KEEP READING FOR A SNEAK PEEK!

SUMMER VACATION AND THE THIEF

I glared at Olivia Stanger's picture on the for-sale sign. Her silver hair sparkled, and her big smile showed teeth as white as wedding cake frosting. Icky-sticky sweet.

So I karate kicked that sign, the sign that announced she was *selling my cabin*.

The sign swung away, but my foot kept going. I landed in the splits, then pressed my whole body against the grass. The sign swung back but missed my head. I was fast. Cougar fast.

Olivia Stanger had forced a stake into the ground

for her sign. A thin pole stuck out near the top of the stake, forming a backward number seven. The sign with her picture hung from the top of the seven. The icky-sticky-sweet smile was as wide as my head.

Next to me was a big stick, so I held it against the ground and pulled myself out of the splits. We were face-to-face again, me and Olivia Stanger's sign.

So I whacked her face with the stick.

Then I spit on the sign, right by the words that said, "Olivia Stanger, Your Wisconsin Lakeshore Realtor."

"What'd that sign ever do to you?"

The voice was a boy covered in mud. Mud on his hands, on his knees, on his green t-shirt. He stood in the grass a few feet from the gravel driveway.

I looked at the muddy boy, then the sign.

I wished Olivia herself would answer. Because if the for-sale sign were an evil talking sign, she'd say, "Miss Christa Boyd-Adams. I will make sure you'll be home every summer, stuck in arts-and-crafts camps. You'll make paper-bag dresses and sock puppets. WAH HA HA HA!"

From under the mud came the boy's voice again. "You got a problem with that sign?"

"Yeah, I got a problem with this sign. A big problem."

"That lady's face is on signs everywhere around here. I guess some people must like her."

"I guess they do. They must like a thief in a business suit selling their best stuff. The stuff they've had since they were born."

He eyed the cabin up and down. "It's not as nice as the places for sale in Arizona. That's where I'm from. But it's a decent cabin. Does it have an actual bathroom? With a toilet that actually flushes?"

"Of course it has a flushing toilet! It's not a hunting shack. It has electricity and a fireplace and two bedrooms. It even has closets."

He nodded. "Then you'll sell it for a wad of money."

Money. That's what my parents wanted. Money from the sale to pay bills. I'd rather sell our house, which was ten hours from the cabin, in a boring neighborhood with hardly any trees.

"Nobody should buy this place," I said. "If you're honest, you'll tell lookers the truth. Are you honest?"

"Guess so."

My brain had to work fast. Race-car fast. I said, "Bats sneak in the cracks at night and swirl around your head, and if they bite you, you need shots or you die. I've already had six shots and I'm only ten years old!"

"I'm eleven." He offered this fact as if it mattered.

I continued, "We hired thirty-two different bug spray guys, and they all left screaming. We've got *everything*. Bats, squirrels, ants, flies, moles. Centipedes and spiders, too. Sometimes snakes come right up the toilet! We save the spiders because they eat the other bugs."

He shrugged. "I ain't afraid of spiders or snakes."

My dad would split his pants over the word "ain't." He was a history teacher, but you'd think he taught English because of his obsession with words. But the school budget cut my dad, and words don't worry him anymore. Just money. Right before we packed our summer stuff, my parents told us we had to sell the cabin. They couldn't afford a house, two cars, our cabin, and to still save college money for my sister, Amelia, and me.

I told the boy, "I'm not afraid of spiders, either. Even poisonous spiders. And I'm not afraid of snakes. I just don't like them."

The boy said, "I really don't have fears. Just born without them, I guess."

"You afraid of that house?" I pointed to the white two-story house where Mr. Edmund Clark lived, only a few hundred feet from our driveway. My parents made me say "mister" or "missus" when talking to old people, and Mr. Edmund Clark was old. He had a stiff leg and flabby face and silver hair like Olivia Stanger. He should probably have married Olivia Stanger since they were both mean and Mrs. Edmund Clark was dead.

Mud boy said, "Why would I be afraid of that house?"

"The guy there is mean and older than fossils."

His hands sprang to his hips. "That old guy is my grandpa."

"You mean your *grump*a?" I laughed, but he didn't.

Mud boy marched toward me with fists ready to spring. I karate kicked the air to show him I meant business. Then he laughed. "Do you know how stupid you look when you do that?"

"Do not!"

I held my arms ready to karate chop. He laughed even harder. He did this crazy spin-around karate kick with his arms waving. Then he stopped and held *his* arms ready to karate chop. We circled each other.

"I have a karate belt," he said.

"Me, too," I said.

"I also have a Judo belt," he said, circling some more.

I'd never heard of a Judo belt, but it sounded way better than a karate belt.

"Me, too," I said, circling some more.

"I punched gangster Al Capone in the stomach," he said.

"Me, too," I said. "Punched Al and his entire gang. Punched 'em all."

He stopped circling and stomped his foot. "Liar! Al Capone has been dead for like a hundred years! I know because he had a house down the road, and my grandpa's been there."

My lips sealed tight because I didn't know who Al Capone was or that he was dead or that Mr. Edmund Clark had been to his house.

Mud boy said, "I lied and said I punched him to prove *you* were lying." He sure looked proud of himself.

I'd been tricked. Now it was liar against liar. Because if the grump was his gramps, why hadn't I seen this kid before?

We stared at each other, karate-style. Judo-style.

Finally he said, "Your hair's really short for a girl."

That's what girls at school said—my hair's too

short and my clothes don't match. My cabin was supposed to be a fashion-free zone. "I don't have time for braids and ponytails. You got a problem with that?"

He thought about it. Then he dropped his karate arms. "I got a bucket of mud. I'm mixing up some mud pies."

"Mud pies?"

"Mud pies. Ten points for hitting that sign from here. Twenty bonus points for hitting her nose."

I was leading 80–40 when Dad shut down the contest. He looked at Olivia Stanger's face on that sign. Bits of grass clung to her silver waves, and her pretty violet-blue eyes were covered with mud. He shook his head and sighed.

Dad went into the cabin and came back with sponges and a bucket of soapy water. He set the bucket by our feet. "Looks like you and your friend have some work to do."

"If I ain't her friend, do I still have to clean this up?"

Ain't! Dad did not split his pants. He said, "Good question. Who are you?"

"Alex Clark."

"Ed's grandson?"

"And Neil and Sally Clark's son. We're buying the house and Grandpa's pizza restaurant so Grandpa can retire." Alex looked at me. "I can eat pizza anytime I want."

"Me, too," I said. "And brownies. Whenever I want."

Dad said, "No you can't, Christa. Now get busy."

We got busy, but I couldn't stop thinking about the stuff Dad and Mom were probably saying inside the cabin. I didn't even need to eavesdrop because I'd heard it all before.

Mom: *Christa, why can't you think before you act?*

Dad: *Christa, that's immature behavior.*

Mom: *Christa, you need to make better choices.*

Dad: *Christa, why can't you act your age?*

Someday I'll be sixteen like Amelia, and maybe then my parents will say things like, *I can't believe you're driving* and *our baby's growing up* and *you'll be graduating before we know it*. That's what they said to her. Seems like Amelia was always growing up too fast, and I was always growing up too slow. Too bad there wasn't a middle child who could've been just right.

When the sign was clean, Alex and I stood back and looked at our work.

"I liked it better before," he said.

Me, too. I scooped a glob of mud on my finger. Nobody was looking, far as I could tell. I rushed to the sign and did the job quick.

And there she was: cabin-thief Olivia Stanger. Big smile, front teeth blacked out.